Cab and Caboose

Kirk Munroe

Contents

CHAPTER I. "RAILROAD BLAKE." 10
CHAPTER II. A RACE FOR THE RAILROAD CUP. 13
CHAPTER III. A CRUEL ACCUSATION. 16
CHAPTER IV. STARTING INTO THE WORLD. 19
CHAPTER V. CHOOSING A CAREER. 21
CHAPTER VI. SMILER, THE RAILROAD DOG. 24
CHAPTER VII. ROD, SMILER, AND THE TRAMP. 27
CHAPTER VIII. EARNING A BREAKFAST. 33
CHAPTER IX. GAINING A FOOTHOLD. 36
CHAPTER X. A THRILLING EXPERIENCE. 39
CHAPTER XI. A BATTLE WITH TRAMPS. 41
CHAPTER XII. BOUND, GAGGED, AND A PRISONER. 44
CHAPTER XIII. HOW BRAKEMAN JOE WAS SAVED. 47
CHAPTER XIV. THE SUPERINTENDENT INVESTIGATES. 50
CHAPTER XV. SMILER TO THE RESCUE. 53
CHAPTER XVI. SNYDER APPLEBY'S JEALOUSY. 56
CHAPTER XVII. ROD AS A BRAKEMAN. 60
CHAPTER XVIII. WORKING FOR A PROMOTION. 62
CHAPTER XIX. THE EXPRESS SPECIAL. 64
CHAPTER XX. TROUBLE IN THE MONEY CAR. 68
CHAPTER XXI. OVER THE TOP OF THE TRAIN. 71
CHAPTER XXII. STOP THIEF! 74
CHAPTER XXIII. A RACE OF LOCOMOTIVES. 77
CHAPTER XXIV. ARRESTED ON SUSPICION. 80
CHAPTER XXV. THE TRAIN ROBBER LEARNS OF ROD'S ARREST. 83
CHAPTER XXVI. A WELCOME VISITOR. 85
CHAPTER XXVII. THE SHERIFF IS INTERVIEWED. 88
CHAPTER XXVIII. LIGHT DAWNS UPON THE SITUATION. 91
CHAPTER XXIX. AN ARRIVAL OF FRIENDS AND ENEMIES. 94
CHAPTER XXX. WHERE ARE THE DIAMONDS? 96
CHAPTER XXXI. ONE HUNDRED MILES AN HOUR! 100
CHAPTER XXXII. SNATCHING VICTORY FROM DEFEAT. 102
CHAPTER XXXIII. A WRECKING TRAIN. 105
CHAPTER XXXIV. ROD ACCEPTS THE LEGACY. 108
CHAPTER XXXV. FIRING ON NUMBER 10. 111
CHAPTER XXXVI. THE ONLY CHANCE OF SAVING THE SPECIAL. 114
CHAPTER XXXVII. INDEPENDENCE OR PRIDE 118
CHAPTER XXXVIII. A MORAL VICTORY. 121
CHAPTER XXXIX. SNYDER IS FORGIVEN. 123

CAB AND CABOOSE

BY

Kirk Munroe

CAB AND CABOOSE

The Story of a Railroad Boy

by

KIRK MUNROE

OFFICERS OF THE NATIONAL COUNCIL

TO THE PUBLIC:--

In the execution of its purpose to give educational value and moral worth to the recreational activities of the boyhood of America, the leaders of the Boy Scout Movement quickly learned that to effectively carry out its program, the boy must be influenced not only in his out-of-door life but also in the diversions of his other leisure moments. It is at such times that the boy is captured by the tales of daring enterprises and adventurous good times. What now is needful is not that his taste should be thwarted but trained. There should constantly be presented to him the books the boy likes best, yet always the books that will be best for the boy. As a matter of fact, however, the boy's taste is being constantly vitiated and exploited by the great mass of cheap juvenile literature.

To help anxiously concerned parents and educators to meet this grave peril, the Library Commission of the Boy Scouts of America has been organized. EVERY BOY'S LIBRARY is the result of their labors. All the books chosen have been approved by them. The Commission is composed of the following members: George F. Bowerman, Librarian, Public Library of the District of Columbia, Washington, D. C.; Harrison W. Graver, Librarian, Carnegie Library of Pittsburgh, Pa.; Claude G. Leland, Superintendent, Bureau of Libraries, Board of Education, New York City; Edward F. Stevens, Librarian, Pratt Institute Free Library, Brooklyn, New York; together with the Editorial Board of our Movement, William D. Murray, George D. Pratt and Frank Presbrey, with Franklin K. Mathiews, Chief Scout Librarian, as Secretary.

"DO A GOOD TURN DAILY."

In selecting the books, the Commission has chosen only such as are of interest to boys, the first twenty-five being either works of fiction or stirring stories of adventurous experiences. In later lists, books of a more serious sort will be included. It is hoped that as many as twenty-five may be added to the Library each year.

Thanks are due the several publishers who have helped to inaugurate this new department of our work. Without their co-operation in making available for popular priced editions some of the best books ever published for boys, the promotion of EVERY BOY'S LIBRARY would have been impossible.

We wish, too, to express our heartiest gratitude to the Library Commission, who, without compensation, have placed their vast experience and immense resources at the service of our Movement.

The Commission invites suggestions as to future books to be included in the Library. Librarians, teachers, parents, and all others interested in welfare work for boys, can render a unique service by forwarding to National Headquarters lists of such books as in their judgment would be suitable for EVERY BOY'S LIBRARY.

Signed James E. West
Chief Scout Executive.

CAB AND CABOOSE: THE STORY OF A RAILROAD BOY.
CHAPTER I.
"RAILROAD BLAKE."

Go it, Rod! You've got to go! One more spurt and you'll have him! There you are over the line! On time! On railroad time! Three cheers for Railroad Blake, fellows! 'Rah, 'rah, 'rah, and a tigah! Good for you, Rod Blake! the cup is yours. It was the prettiest race ever seen on the Euston track, and 'Cider' got so badly left that he cut off and went to the dressing-room without finishing. Billy Bliss was a good second, though, and you only beat him by a length."

Amid a thousand such cries as these, from the throats of the excited boys and a furious waving of hats, handkerchiefs, and ribbon-decked parasols from the grand stand, the greatest bicycling event of the year so far as Euston was concerned, was finished, and Rodman Blake was declared winner of the Railroad Cup. It was the handsomest thing of the kind ever seen in that part of the country, and had been presented to the Steel Wheel Club of Euston by President Vanderveer of the great New York and Western Railroad, who made his summer home at that place. The race for this trophy was the principal event at the annual meet of the club, which always took place on the first Wednesday of September. If any member won it three years in succession it was to be his to keep, and every winner was entitled to have his name engraved on it.

Snyder Appleby or "Cider Apples" as the boys, with their love for nicknames, sometimes called him, had won it two years in succession, and was confident of doing the same thing this year. He had just obtained, through President Vanderveer, a position in the office of the Railroad Company, and only waited to ride this last race for the "Railroad Cup," as it was called in honor of its donor, before going to the city and entering upon his new duties.

Now to be beaten so badly, and by that young upstart, for so he called Rod Blake, was a mortification almost too great to be borne. As Snyder left the track without finishing the last race and made his way to the dressing-room under the grand stand, he ground his teeth, and vowed to get even with his victorious rival yet. The cheers and yells of delight with which the fellows were hailing the victor, made him feel his defeat all the more bitterly, and seek the more eagerly for some plan for that victor's humiliation.

Snyder Appleby was generally considered by the boys as one of the meanest fellows in Euston, and that is the reason why they called him "Cider Apples"; for those, as everybody knows, are most always the very poorest of the picking. So the name seemed to be appropriate, as well as a happy parody on that to which he was really entitled. He was the son, or rather the adopted son, of Major Arms Appleby, who, next to President Vanderveer, was the richest man in Euston, and lived in the great, rambling stone mansion that had been in his family for generations.

The Major, who was a bachelor, was also one of the kindest-hearted, most generous, and most obstinate of men. He loved to do good deeds; but he loved to do them in his own way, and his way was certain to be the one that was contrary to the advice of everybody else. Thus it happened that he determined to adopt the year-old baby boy who was left on his doorstep one stormy night, a little more than sixteen years before this story opens. He was not fond of babies, nor did he care to have children about him. Simply because everybody advised him to send this one to the county house, where it might be cared for by the proper authorities, he declared he would do nothing of the kind; but would adopt the little waif and bring him up as his own son.

As the boy grew, and developed many undesirable traits of character, Major Appleby was too kind-hearted to see them, and too obstinate to be warned against them.

"Don't tell me," he would say, "I know more about the boy than anybody else, and am fully capable of forming my opinion concerning him."

Thus Snyder Appleby, as he was called, because the name "Snyder" was found marked on the basket in which he had been left at the Major's door, grew up with the fixed idea that if he only pleased his adopted father he might act about as he chose with everybody else. Now he was nearly eighteen years of age, big and strong, with a face that, but for its coarseness, would have been called handsome. He was fond of display, did everything for effect, was intolerably lazy, had no idea of the word punctuality, and never kept an engagement unless he felt inclined to do so. He always had plenty of pocket money which he spent lavishly, and was not without a certain degree of popularity among the other boys of Euston. He had subscribed more largely than anybody else to the Steel Wheel Club upon its formation, and had thus succeeded in having himself elected its captain.

As he was older and stronger than any of the other members who took up racing, and as he always rode the lightest and best wheel that money could procure, he had, without much hard work, easily maintained a lead in the racing field, and had come to consider himself as invincible. He regarded himself as such a sure winner of this last race for the Railroad Cup, that he had not taken the trouble to go into training for it. He would not even give up his cigarette smoking, a habit that he had acquired because he considered it fashionable and manly. Now he was beaten, disgracefully, and that by a boy nearly two years younger than himself. It was too much, and he determined to find some excuse for his defeat, that should at the same time remove the disgrace from him, and place it upon other shoulders.

Rodman Ray Blake, or R. R. Blake as he signed his name, and "Railroad Blake" as the boys often called him, was Major Appleby's nephew, and the son of his only sister. She had married an impecunious young artist against her brother's wish, on which account he had declined ever to see her again. When she died, after two years of poverty-stricken widowhood, she left a loving, forgiving letter for her brother, and in it committed her darling boy to his charge. If she had not done this, but had trusted to his generous impulses, all would have gone well, and the events that serve to make up this story would never have taken place. As it was, the Major, feeling that the boy was forced upon him, was greatly aggrieved. That the lad should bear a remarkable resemblance to his handsome artist father also irritated him. As a result, while he really became very fond of the boy, and was never unkind to him, he treated him with an assumed indifference that was keenly felt by the loving, high-spirited lad. As for Snyder Appleby, he was jealous of Rodman from the very first; and when, only a short time before the race meeting of the Steel Wheel Club, the latter was almost unanimously elected to his place as captain, this feeling was greatly increased.

CHAPTER II.
A RACE FOR THE RAILROAD CUP.

Young Blake had now been in Euston two years, and was, among the boys, decidedly the most popular fellow in the place. He was a slightly-built chap; but with muscles like steel wires, and possessed of wonderful agility and powers of endurance. He excelled in all athletic sports, was a capital boxer, and at the same time found little difficulty in maintaining a good rank in his classes. He had taken to bicycling from the very first, and quickly became an expert rider, though he had never gone in for racing. It was therefore a great surprise, even to his friends, when, on the very day before the race meeting, he entered his name for the event that was to result in the winning or losing of the Railroad Cup. It would not have been so much of a surprise had anybody known of his conversation, a few weeks before, with Eltje Vanderveer, the railroad president's only daughter. She was a few months younger than Rod, and ever since he had jumped into the river to save her pet kitten from drowning, they had been fast friends.

So, when in talking of the approaching meeting, Eltje had said, "How I wish you were a racer, and could win our cup, Rod," the boy instantly made up his mind to try for it. He only answered, "Do you? Well, perhaps I may go in for that sort of thing some time."

Then he began training, so secretly that nobody but Dan, a stable boy on his uncle's place and Rod's most ardent admirer, was aware of it; but with such steady determination that on the eventful day of the great race his physical condition was very nearly perfect.

He was on hand at the race track bright and early; for, as captain of the club, Rod had a great deal to do in seeing that everything went smoothly, and in starting on time the dozen events that preceded the race for the Railroad Cup, which came last on the programme.

While these earlier events were being run off Snyder Appleby, faultlessly at-
tired, sat in the grand stand beside his adopted father, and directly behind President
Vanderveer and his pretty daughter, to whom he tried to render himself especially
agreeable. He listened respectfully to the Major's stories, made amusing comments
on the racers for Eltje's benefit, and laughed heartily at the puns that her father was
given to making.

"But how about your own race, Mr. Appleby?" asked Eltje. "Don't you feel any
anxiety concerning it? It is to be the hardest one of all, isn't it?"

Immensely flattered at being addressed as Mister Appleby, Snyder replied carelessly, "Oh, yes! of course I am most anxious to win it, especially as you are here to
see it run; but I don't anticipate much difficulty. Bliss is a hard man to beat; but I
have done it before, and I guess I can do it again."

"Then you don't think Rodman has any chance of winning?"

"Well, hardly. You see this is his first race, and experience goes a long way in
such affairs. Still, he rides well, and it wouldn't surprise me to see him make a good
third at the finish."

Eltje smiled as she answered, "Perhaps he will finish third; but it would surprise me greatly to see him do so."

This pretty girl, with the Dutch name, had such faith in her friend Rod, that
she did not believe he would ever be third, or even second, where he had once
made up his mind to be first.

Failing to catch her real meaning, Snyder replied: "Of course he may not do as
well as that; but he ought to. As captain of the club he ought to sustain the honor of
his position, you know. If he doesn't feel able to take at least third place in a five-
starter race, he should either resign, or keep out of the racing field altogether. Now
I must leave you; for I see I am wanted. You'll wish me good luck, won't you?"

"Yes," answered Eltje mischievously, "I wish you all the luck you deserve."

Forced to be content with this answer, but wondering if there was any hidden meaning in it, Snyder left the grand stand, and strolled leisurely around to the
dressing-room, lighting a cigarette as he went.

"Hurry up!" shouted Rod, who was the soul of punctuality and was particularly
anxious that all the events of this, his first race meeting, should be started on time.
"Hurry up. Our race will be called in five minutes, and you've barely time to dress

for it."

"Where's my wheel?" asked Snyder, glancing over the dozen or more machines stacked at one side of the room, but without seeing his own.

"I haven't seen it," answered Rod, "but I supposed you had left it in some safe place."

"So I did. I left it in the club house, where there would be no chance of anybody tampering with it; for I've heard of such things happening, but I ordered Dan to have it down here in time for the race."

"Do you mean to insinuate--" began Rod hotly; but controlling himself, he continued more calmly, "I didn't know that you had given Dan any orders, and I sent him over to the house on an errand a few minutes ago. Never mind, though, I'll go for your machine myself, and have it here by the time you are dressed."

Without waiting for a reply, the young captain started off on a run, while his adopted cousin began leisurely to undress, and get into his racing costume. By the time he was ready, Rod had returned leading the beautiful machine, which he had not ridden for fear lest some accident might happen to it.

Then the race was called, and a pistol shot sent the five young athletes bending low over their handle-bars spinning down the course. They all wore the club colors of scarlet and white; but from Rod's bicycle fluttered the bit of blue ribbon that Dan had been sent to the young captain's room to get, and which he had hastily knotted to the handle-bar of his machine just before starting. Eltje Vanderveer smiled and flushed slightly as she noticed it, and then all her attention was concentrated upon the varying fortunes of the flying wheelmen.

It was a five-mile race, and therefore a test of endurance rather than of strength or skill. There were two laps to the mile, and for seven of these Snyder Appleby held an easy lead. His name was heard above all others in the cheering that greeted each passing of the grand stand, though the others were encouraged to stick to him and not give it up yet. That two of them had no intention of giving it up, was shown at the end of the eighth lap, when the three leading wheels whirled past the grand stand so nearly abreast that no advantage could be claimed for either one.

Now the cheering was tremendous; but the names of Rod Blake and Billy Bliss were tossed from mouth to mouth equally with that of Snyder Appleby. At the end of nine laps the champion of two years had fallen hopelessly behind. His face wore a distressed look, and his breath came in painful gasps. Cigarettes had done their work with him, and his wind was gone. The two leaders were still abreast; but Rod had obtained the inside position, and if he could keep up the pace the race was his.

Eltje Vanderveer's face was pale, and her hands were clinched with the intense excitement of the moment. Was her champion to win after all? Was her bit of blue ribbon to be borne triumphantly to the front? Inch by inch it creeps into a lead. Now they are coming down the home stretch. The speed of that last spurt is wonderful. Nothing like it has ever been seen at the wind-up of a five-mile race on the Euston track. Looking at them, head on, it is for a few seconds hard to tell which is leading. Then a solitary shout for Rod Blake is heard. In another moment it has swelled into a perfect roar of cheering, and there is a tempest of tossing hats, handkerchiefs, and parasols.

Rod Blake has won by a length, Billy Bliss is second, Snyder Appleby was such a bad third that he has gone to the dressing-room without finishing, and the others are nowhere.

The speed of the winning wheels cannot be checked at once, and as they go shooting on past the stand, the exhausted riders are seen to reel in their saddles. They would have fallen but for the willing hands outstretched to receive them. Dan is the first to reach the side of his adored young master, and as the boy drops into his arms, the faithful fellow says:

"You've won it, Mister Rod! You've won it fair and square; but you want to look out for Mister Snyder. I heerd him a-saying bad things about you when he passed me on that last lap, and I'm afeard he means some kind of mischief."

CHAPTER III.
A CRUEL ACCUSATION.

The attention of the spectators, including the club members, was so entirely given to the finish of the famous race for the Railroad Cup, that, for a few minutes Snyder Appleby was the sole occupant of the dressing-room. When a group of the fellows, forming a sort of triumphal escort to the victors, noisily entered it, they found him standing by his machine. It was supported by two rests placed under its handle bars, and he was gazing curiously at the big wheel, which he was slowly spinning with one hand.

"Hello, 'Cider'!" cried the first of the new-comers, "what's up? Anything the matter with your wheel?"

"I believe there is," answered the ex-captain, in such a peculiar tone of voice that it at once arrested attention. "I don't know what is wrong, and I wouldn't make an examination until some of you fellows came in. In a case like this I believe in having plenty of witnesses and doing everything openly."

"What do you mean?" asked one of the group, whose noisy entrance was now succeeded by a startled silence.

"Turn that wheel and you'll see what I mean," replied Snyder.

"Why, it turns as hard as though it were running on plain bearing that had never been oiled!" exclaimed the member who had undertaken to turn the wheel as requested.

"That's just it, and I don't think it's very surprising that I failed to win the race with a wheel in that condition, do you?"

"Indeed I do not. The only surprising thing is that you held the lead so long as you did, and managed to come in third. I know I couldn't have run a single lap if I'd been on that wheel. What's the matter with it? Wasn't it all right when you started?"

"I thought it was," replied Snyder, "but I soon found that something was wrong, and before I left the track it was all I could do to move it. Now, I want you fellows to find out what the matter is."

A few moments of animated discussion followed, while several of the fellows made a careful examination of the bicycle.

"Great Scott!" exclaimed one; "what's in this oil cup? It looks as though it were choked with black sand."

"It's emery powder!" cried another, extracting a few grains of the black, oil-soaked stuff on the point of a knife blade. "No wonder your wheel won't turn. How on earth did it get there?"

"That is what I would like to find out," answered the owner of the machine. "It certainly was not there when I left the club house; for I had just gone over every part and assured myself that it was in perfect order. Since then but two persons have touched it, and I am one of them. I don't think it likely that anybody will charge me with having done this thing, seeing that my sole interest was to win the race, and that if I so nearly succeeded with my wheel in this condition, I could easily have done so had it been all right. Nothing could be more painful to me than to bring a charge against one who lives under the same roof that I do; but you all know who had the greatest interest in having me lose this race. I think you all know, too, that he is the only person besides myself who handled my wheel immediately before it. The one whom I trusted to bring it here in safety was sent off by this person on some frivolous errand at the last moment. Then, neglecting other and important duties, he volunteered to get the machine himself. He was gone before I had a chance to decline his offer. That is all I have to say upon this most unpleasant subject, and I should not have said so much had not my own reputation, both as a racing man and a gentleman, been at stake. Now I place the whole affair in the hands of the club, satisfied that they will do me justice."

Rod Blake, seated on a camp-stool, with a heavy "sweater" thrown over his shoulders, and slowly recovering from the exhaustion of the race, had observed and listened to all this with a pained curiosity. He could not believe any member of the club guilty of such a cowardly act. When Snyder began to charge him with having committed it, his face became deadly pale, and he gazed at his adopted cousin with an expression akin to terror. As the latter finished, the young captain sprang to his feet, exclaiming:

"Snyder Appleby, how dare you bring such an accusation against me? You know I am incapable of doing such a thing! Your wheel was in perfect condition when I delivered it to you, and you know it was."

"I can easily believe that the fellow who would perform the act would be equally ready to lie out of it," replied Snyder.

"Do you mean that I lie?"

"That is about the size of it."

This was more than the hot-tempered young athlete could bear; and almost before the words were out of Snyder's mouth, a blow delivered with all the nervous force of Rodman's right arm sent him staggering back. It would have laid him on the floor, had not several of the fellows caught him in their arms.

He was furious with rage, and would have sprung at Rodman had he not been restrained. As it was, he hissed through his clinched teeth, "I'll make you suffer for this yet, see if I don't."

Immediately after delivering the blow, Rod turned, without a word, and began putting on his clothes. The fellows watched him in silence. A minute later he was dressed, and stood in the doorway. Here he turned and said:

"I am going home, fellows, and I shall wait there just one hour for an assurance that you have faith in me, and do not believe a word of this horrible charge. If such a message, sent by the whole club, reaches me within that time, I will undertake to prove my innocence. If it does not come, then I cease, not only to be your captain, but a member of the club."

CHAPTER IV.
STARTING INTO THE WORLD.

As Rod finished speaking he left the room and walked away. He had hardly disappeared, and the fellows were still looking at each other in a bewildered fashion, when a message was sent in. It was that President Vanderveer, who was distributing the prizes for the several races out in front of the grand stand, was ready to present the Railroad Cup to Rodman Blake, and wanted him to come and receive it. Then somebody went out and whispered to the President. Excusing himself for a moment to the throng of spectators, he visited the dressing-room, where he heard the whole story. It was hurriedly told; but he comprehended enough of it to know that the cup could not, at that moment, be presented to anybody. So he went back, and with a very sober face, told the people that owing to circumstances which he was not at liberty to explain just then, it was impossible to award the Railroad Cup at that meeting.

The crowd slowly melted away; but before they left, everybody had heard one version or another of the story told to President Vanderveer in the dressing-room. Some believed Rod to be innocent of the charge brought against him, and some believed him guilty. Almost all of them said it was a pity that such races could not be won and lost honestly, and there must be some fire where there was so much smoke; and they told each other how they had noticed from the very first that something was wrong with Snyder Appleby's wheel.

Major Appleby heard the story, first from President Vanderveer, and afterwards from his adopted son, who confirmed it by displaying the side of his face which was swollen and bruised from Rodman's blow. Fully believing what Snyder told him, the Major became very angry. He declared that no such disgrace had ever before been brought to his house, and that the boy who was the cause of it could no longer be sheltered by his roof. In vain did people talk to him, and urge him to reflect before he acted. He had decided upon his course, and the more they advised him, the more determined he became not to be moved from it.

While he was thus storming and fuming outside the dressing-room, the members of the wheel club were holding a meeting behind its closed door. Did they believe Rodman Blake guilty of the act charged against him or did they not? The debate was a long and exciting one; but the question was finally decided in his favor. They did not believe him capable of doing anything so mean. They would make a thorough investigation of the affair, and aid him by every means in their power to prove his innocence.

This was the purport of the message sent to the young captain by the club secretary, Billy Bliss; but it was sent too late. The members had taken no note of time in the heat of their discussion, and the hour named by Rodman had already elapsed before Billy Bliss started on his errand. The fellows did not think a few minutes more or less would make any difference, though they urged the secretary to hurry and deliver his message as quickly as possible. A few minutes however did make all the difference in the world to Rod Blake. With him an hour meant exactly sixty minutes; and when Billy Bliss reached Major Appleby's house the boy whom he sought was nowhere to be found.

Major Appleby and his adopted son walked home together, the former full of wrath at what he believed to be the disgraceful action of his nephew, and the latter secretly rejoicing at it. On reaching the house, the Major went at once to Rodman's room where he found the boy gazing from the window, with a hard, defiant, expression on his face. He was longing for a single loving word; for a mother's sympathetic ear into which he might pour his griefs; but his pride was prepared to withstand any harshness, as well as to resent the faintest suspicion of injustice.

"Well, sir," began the Major, "what have you to say for yourself? and how do you explain this disgraceful affair?"

"I cannot explain it, Uncle; but----"

"That will do, sir. If you cannot explain it, I want to hear nothing further. What I do want, however, is that you shall so arrange your future plans that you may no longer be dependent on my roof for shelter. Here is sufficient money for your immediate needs. As my sister's child you have a certain claim on me. This I shall be willing to honor to the extent of providing you against want, whenever you have settled upon your mode of life, and choose to favor me with your future address. The sooner you can decide upon your course of action the better." Thus saying the kind-hearted, impetuous, and wrong-headed old Major laid a roll of bills on the table, and left the room.

Fifteen minutes later, or five minutes before Billy Bliss reached the house, Rod Blake also left the room. The roll of bills lay untouched where his uncle had placed it, and he carried only his M. I. P. or bicycle travelling bag, containing the pictures of his parents, a change of underclothing, and a few trifles that were absolutely his own. He passed out of the house by a side door, and was seen but by one person as he plunged into the twilight shadows of the park. Thus, through the gathering darkness, the poor boy, proud, high-spirited, and, as he thought, friendless, set forth alone, to fight his battle with the world.

CHAPTER V.
CHOOSING A CAREER.

As Rod Blake, heavy-hearted, and weary, both mentally and physically from his recent struggles, left his uncle's house, he felt utterly reckless, and paid no heed to the direction his footsteps were taking. His one idea was to get away as quickly, and as far as possible, from those who had treated him so cruelly. "If only the fellows had stood by me," he thought, "I might have stayed and fought it out. But to have them go back on me, and take Snyder's word in preference to mine, is too much."

Had the poor boy but known that Billy Bliss was even then hastening to bear a message of good-will and confidence in him from the "fellows" how greatly his burden of trial would have been lightened. But he did not know, and so he pushed blindly on, suffering as much from his own hasty and ill-considered course of action, as from the more deliberate cruelty of his adopted cousin. At length he came to the brow of a steep slope leading down to the railroad, the very one of which Eltje's father was president. The railroad had always possessed a fascination for him, and he had often sat on this bank watching the passing trains, wondering at their speed, and speculating as to their destinations. He had frequently thought he should like to lead the life of a railroad man, and had been pleased when the fellows called him "Railroad Blake" on account of his initials. Now, this idea presented itself to him again more strongly than ever.

An express train thundered by. The ruddy glow from the furnace door of its locomotive, which was opened at that moment, revealed the engineman seated in the cab, with one hand on the throttle lever, and peering steadily ahead through the gathering gloom. What a glorious life he led! So full of excitement and constant change. What a power he controlled. How easy it was for him to fly from whatever was unpleasant or trying. As these thoughts flashed through the boy's mind, the red lights at the rear of the train seemed to blink pleasantly at him, and invite him to follow them.

"I will," he cried, springing to his feet. "I will follow wherever they may lead me. Why should I not be a railroad man as well as another? They have all been boys and all had to begin some time."

At this moment he was startled by a sound of a voice close beside him saying, "Supper is ready, Mister Rod." It was Dan the stable boy; and, as Rodman asked him, almost angrily, how he dared follow him without orders, and what he was spying out his movements for, he replied humbly: "I ain't a-spying on you, Mister Rod, and I only followed you to tell you supper was ready, 'cause I thought maybe you didn't know it."

"Well, I didn't and it makes no difference whether I did or not," said Rod. "I have left my uncle's house for good and all, Dan, and there are no more suppers in it for me."

"I was afeard so! I was afeard so, Mister Rod," exclaimed the boy with a real distress in his voice, "an' to tell the truth that's why I came after you. I couldn't a-bear to have you go without saying good-by, and I thought maybe, perhaps, you'd let me go along with you. Please do, Mister Rod. I'll work for you and serve you faithfully, an' I'd a heap rather go on a tramp, or any place along with you, than stay here without you. Please, Mister Rod."

"No, Dan, it would be impossible to take you with me," said Rodman, who was deeply touched by this proof of his humble friend's loyalty. "It will be all I can do to find work for myself; but I'm grateful to you all the same for showing that you still think well of me. It's a great thing, I can tell you, for a fellow in my position to know that he leaves even one friend behind him when he is forced to go away from his only home."

"You leaves a-plenty of them--a-plenty!" interrupted the stable boy eagerly. "I heerd Miss Eltje telling her father that it was right down cruel not to give you the cup, an' that you couldn't do a thing, such as they said, any more than she could, or he could himself. An' her father said no more did he believe you could, an' you'd come out of it all right yet. Miss Eltje was right up an' down mad about it, she was. Oh, I tell you, Mister Rod, you've got a-plenty of friends; an' if you'll only stay you'll find 'em jest a-swarmin'."

At this Rodman laughed outright, and said: "Dan, you are a fine fellow, and you have done me good already. Now what I want you to do is just to stay here and discover some more friends for me. I will manage to let you know what I am do-ing; but you must not tell anybody a word about me, nor where I am, nor anything. Now good-by, and mind, don't say a word about having seen me, unless Miss Eltje should happen to ask you. If she should, you might say that I shall always remember her, and be grateful to her for believing in me. Good-by."

With this Rod plunged down the steep bank to the railroad track, and disap-peared in the darkness. He went in the direction of the next station to Euston, about five miles away, as he did not wish to be recognized when he made the attempt to secure a ride on some train to New York. It was to be an attempt only; for he had not a cent of money in his pockets, and had no idea of how he should obtain the coveted ride. In addition to being penniless, he was hungry, and his hunger was increased tenfold by the knowledge that he had no means of satisfying it. Still he was a boy with unlimited confidence in himself. He always had fallen on his feet; and, though this was the worse fix in which he had ever found himself, he had faith that he would come out of it all right somehow. His heart was already so much lighter since he had learned from Dan that some of his friends, and especially Eltje Vanderveer, still believed in him, that his situation did not seem half so desperate as it had an hour before.

Rod was already enough of a railroad man to know that, as he was going east, he must walk on the west bound track. By so doing he would be able to see trains bound west, while they were still at some distance from him, and would be in no danger from those bound east and overtaking him.

When he was about half a mile from the little station, toward which he was walking, he heard the long-drawn, far-away whistle of a locomotive. Was it ahead of him or behind? On account of the bewildering echoes he could not tell. To settle the question he kneeled down, and placed his ear against one of rails of the west bound track. It was cold and silent. Then he tried the east bound track in the same way. This rail seemed to tingle with life, and a faint, humming sound came from it. It was a perfect railroad telephone, and it informed the listener as plainly as words could have told him, that a train was approaching from the west.

He stopped to note its approach. In a few minutes the rails of the east bound track began to quiver with light from the powerful reflector in front of its locomotive. Then they stretched away toward the oncoming train in gleaming bands of indefinite length, while the dazzling light seemed to cut a bright pathway between walls of solid blackness for the use of the advancing monster. As the bewildering glare passed him, Rod saw that the train was a long, heavy-laden freight, and that some of its cars contained cattle. He stood motionless as it rushed past him, shaking the solid earth with its ponderous weight, and he drew a decided breath of relief at the sight of the blinking red eyes on the rear platform of its caboose. How he wished he was in that caboose, riding comfortably toward New York, instead of plodding wearily along on foot, with nothing but uncertainties ahead of him.

CHAPTER VI.
SMILER, THE RAILROAD DOG.

As Rod stood gazing at the receding train he noticed a human figure step from the lighted interior of the caboose, through the open doorway, to the platform, apparently kick at something, and almost instantly return into the car. At the same time the boy fancied he heard a sharp cry of pain; but was not sure. As he resumed his tiresome walk, gazing longingly after the vanishing train lights, he saw another light, a white one that moved toward him with a swinging motion, close to the ground. While he was wondering what it was, he almost stumbled over a small animal that stood motionless on the track, directly in front of him. It was a dog. Now Rod dearly loved dogs, and seemed instinctively to know that this one was in some sort of trouble. As he stopped to pat it, the creature uttered a little whine, as though asking his sympathy and help. At the same time it licked his hand.

While he was kneeling beside the dog and trying to discover what its trouble was, the swinging white light approached so closely that he saw it to be a lantern, borne by a man who, in his other hand, carried a long-handled iron wrench. He was the track-walker of that section, who was obliged to inspect every foot of the eight miles of track under his charge, at least twice a day; and the wrench was for the tightening of any loose rail joints that he might discover.

"Hello!" exclaimed this individual as he came before the little group, and held his lantern so as to get a good view of them. "What's the matter here?"

"I have just found this dog," replied Rod, "and he seems to be in pain. If you will please hold your light a little closer perhaps I can see what has happened to him."

The man did as requested, and Rod uttered an exclamation of pleasure as the light fell full upon the dog; for it was the finest specimen of a bull terrier he had ever seen. It was white and brindled, its chest was of unusual breadth, and its square jaws indicated a tenacity of purpose that nothing short of death itself could overcome. Now one of its legs was evidently hurt, and it had an ugly cut under the left ear, from which blood was flowing. Its eyes expressed an almost human intelligence; and, as it looked up at Rod and tried to lick his face, it seemed to say, "I know you will be my friend, and I trust you to help me." About its neck was a leathern collar, bearing a silver plate, on which was inscribed: "Be kind to me, for I am Smiler the Railroad Dog."

"I know this dog," exclaimed the track-walker, as he read these words, "and I reckon every railroad man in the country knows him; or at any rate has heard of him. He used to belong to Andrew Dean, who was killed when his engine went over the bank at Hager's two years ago. He thought the world of the dog, and it used to travel with him most always; only once in a while it would go visiting on some of the other engines. It was off that way when Andrew got killed, and since then it has travelled all over the country, like as though it was hunting for its old master. The dog lives on trains and engines, and railroad men are always glad to see him. Some of them got up this collar for him a while ago. Why, Smiler, old dog, how did you come here in this fix? I never heard of you getting left or falling off a train before."

"I think he must have come from the freight that just passed us," said Rod, "and I shouldn't wonder," he added, suddenly recalling the strange movements of the figure he had seen appear for an instant at the caboose door, "if he was kicked off." Then he described the scene of which he had caught a glimpse as the freight train passed him.

"I'd like to meet the man who'd dare do such a thing," exclaimed the track-walker. "If I wouldn't kick him! He'd dance to a lively tune if any of us railroad chaps got hold of him, I can tell you. It must have been an accident, though; for nobody would hurt Smiler. Now I don't know exactly what to do. Smiler can't be left here, and I'm afraid he isn't able to walk very far. If I had time I'd carry him back to the freight. She's side-tracked only a quarter of a mile from here, waiting for Number 8 to pass. I'm due at Euston inside of an hour, and I don't dare waste any more time."

"I'll take him if you say so," answered Rod, who had been greatly interested in the dog's history. "I believe I can carry him that far."

"All right," replied the track-walker. "I wish you would. You'll have to move lively though; for if Number 8 is on time, as she generally is, you haven't a moment to lose."

"I'll do my best," said the boy, and a moment later he was hurrying down the track with his M. I. P. bag strapped to his shoulders, and with the dog so strangely committed to his care, clasped tightly in his arms. At the same time the track-walker, with his swinging lantern, was making equally good speed in the opposite direction. As Rod rounded a curve, and sighted the lights of the waiting freight train, he heard the warning whistle of Number 8 behind him, and redoubled his exertions. He did not stop even as the fast express whirled past him, though he was nearly blinded by the eddying cloud of dust and cinders that trailed behind it. But, if Number 8 was on time, so was he. Though Smiler had grown heavy as lead in his aching arms, and though his breath was coming in panting gasps, he managed to climb on the rear platform of the caboose, just as the freight was pulling out. How glad he was at that moment of the three weeks training he had just gone through with. It had won him something, even if his name was not to be engraved on the railroad cup of the Steel Wheel Club.

As the boy stood in the rear doorway of the caboose, gazing doubtfully into its interior, a young fellow who looked like a tramp, and who had been lying on one of the cushioned lockers, or benches, that ran along the sides of the car, sprang to his feet with a startled exclamation. At the same moment Smiler drew back his upper lip so as to display a glistening row of teeth, and, uttering a deep growl, tried to escape from Rod's arms.

"What are you doing in this car! and what do you mean by bringing that dog in here?" cried the fellow angrily, at the same time advancing with a threatening gesture. "Come, clear out of here or I'll put you out," he added. The better to defend himself, if he should be attacked, the boy dropped the dog; and, with another fierce growl, forgetful of his hurts, Smiler flew at the stranger's throat.

CHAPTER VII.
ROD, SMILER, AND THE TRAMP.

"Help! Murder! Take off your dog!" yelled the young tramp, throwing up his arm to protect his face from Smiler's attack, and springing backward. In so doing he tripped and fell heavily to the floor, with the dog on top of him, growling savagely, and tearing at the ragged coat-sleeve in which his teeth were fastened. Fearful lest the dog might inflict some serious injury upon the fellow, Rodman rushed to his assistance. He had just seized hold of Smiler, when a kick from the struggling tramp sent his feet flying from under him, and he too pitched headlong. There ensued a scene which would have been comical enough to a spectator, but which was anything but funny to those who took part in it. Over and over they rolled, striking, biting, kicking, and struggling. The tramp was the first to regain his feet; but almost at the same instant Smiler escaped from Rod's embrace, and again flew at him. They had rolled over the caboose floor until they were close to its rear door; and now, with a yell of terror, the tramp darted through it, sprang from the moving train, and disappeared in the darkness, leaving a large piece of his trousers in the dog's mouth. Just then the forward door was opened, and two men with lanterns on their arms, entered the car.

They were Conductor Tobin, and rear-brakeman Joe, his right-hand man, who had just finished switching their train back on the main track, and getting it again started on its way toward New York. At the sight of Rod, who was of course a perfect stranger to them, sitting on the floor, hatless, covered with dust, his clothing bearing many signs of the recent fray, and ruefully feeling of a lump on his forehead that was rapidly increasing in size, and of Smiler whose head was bloody, and who was still worrying the last fragment of clothing that the tramp's rags had yielded him, they stood for a moment in silent bewilderment.

"Well, I'll be blowed!" said Conductor Tobin at length.

"Me too," said Brakeman Joe, who believed in following the lead of his superior officer.

"May I inquire," asked Conductor Tobin, seating himself on a locker close to where Rod still sat on the floor, "May I inquire who you are? and where you came from? and how you got here? and what's happened to Smiler? and what's came of the fellow we left sleeping here a few minutes ago? and what's the meaning of all this business, anyway?"

"Yes, we'd like to know," said the Brakeman, taking a seat on the opposite locker, and regarding the boy with a curiosity that was not unmixed with suspicion. Owing to extensive dealings with tramps, Brakeman Joe was very apt to be suspicious of all persons who were dirty, and ragged, and had bumps on their foreheads.

"The trouble is," replied Rod, looking first at Conductor Tobin and then at Brakeman Joe, "that I don't know all about it myself. Nobody does except the fellow who just left here in such a hurry, and Smiler, who can't tell."

Here the dog, hearing his name mentioned, dragged himself rather stiffly to the boy's side; for now that the excitement was over, his hurts began to be painful again, and licked his face.

"Well, you must be one of the right sort, at any rate," said Conductor Tobin, noting this movement, "for Smiler is a dog that doesn't make friends except with them as are."

"He knows what's what, and who's who," added Brakeman Joe, nodding his head. "Don't you, Smiler, old dog?"

"My name," continued the boy, "is R. R. Blake."

"Railroad Blake?" interrupted Conductor Tobin inquiringly.

"Or 'Runaway Blake'?" asked Brakeman Joe who, still somewhat suspicious, was studying the boy's face and the M. I. P. bag attached to his shoulders.

"Both," answered Rod, with a smile. "The boys where I live, or rather where I did live, often call me 'Railroad Blake,' and I am a runaway. That is, I was turned away first, and ran away afterwards."

Then, as briefly as possible, he gave them the whole history of his adventures, beginning with the bicycle race, and ending with the disappearance of the young tramp through the rear door of the caboose in which they sat. Both men listened with the deepest attention, and without interrupting him save by occasional ejaculations, expressive of wonder and sympathy.

"Well, I'll be blowed!" exclaimed Conductor Tobin, when he had finished; while Brakeman Joe, without a word, went to the rear door and examined the platform, with the hope, as he afterwards explained, of finding there the fellow who had kicked Smiler off the train, and of having a chance to serve him in the same way. Coming back with a disappointed air, he proceeded to light a fire in the little round caboose stove, and prepare a pot of coffee for supper, leaving Rodman's case to be managed by Conductor Tobin as he thought best.

The latter told the boy that the young tramp, as they called him, was billed through to New York, to look after some cattle that were on the train; but that he was a worthless, ugly fellow, who had not paid the slightest attention to them, and whose only object in accepting the job was evidently to obtain a free ride in the caboose. Smiler, whom he had been delighted to find on the train when it was turned over to him, had taken a great dislike to the fellow from the first. He had growled and shown his teeth whenever the tramp moved about the car, and several times the latter had threatened to teach him better manners. When he and Brakeman Joe went to the forward end of the train, to make ready for side-tracking it, they left the dog sitting on the rear platform of the caboose, and the tramp apparently asleep, as

Rod had found him, on one of the lockers. He must have taken advantage of their absence to deal the dog the cruel kick that cut his ear, and landed him, stunned and bruised, on the track where he had been discovered.

"I'm glad he's gone," concluded Conductor Tobin, "for if he hadn't left, we would have fired him for what he did to Smiler. We won't have that dog hurt on this road, not if we know it. It won't hurt him to have to walk to New York, and I don't care if he never gets there. What worries me, though, is who'll look after those cattle, and go down to the stock-yard with them, now that he's gone."

"Why couldn't I do it?" asked Rod eagerly. "I'd be glad to."

"You!" said Conductor Tobin incredulously. "Why, you look like too much of a gentleman to be handling cattle."

"I hope I am a gentleman," answered the boy with a smile; "but I am a very poverty-stricken one just at present, and if I can earn a ride to the city, just by looking after some cattle, I don't know why I shouldn't do that as well as anything else. What I would like to do though, most of all things, is to live up to my nickname, and become a railroad man."

"You would, would you?" said Conductor Tobin. Then, as though he were propounding a conundrum, he asked: "Do you know the difference between a railroad man and a chap who wants to be one?"

"I don't know that I do," answered the boy.

"Well, the difference is, that the latter gets what he deserves, and the former deserves what he gets. What I mean is, that almost anybody who is willing to take whatever job is offered him can get a position on a railroad; but before he gets promoted he will have to deserve it several times over. In other words, it takes more honesty, steadiness, faithfulness, hard work, and brains to work your way up in railroad life than in any other business that I know of. However, at present, you are only going along with me as stockman, in which position I am glad to have you, so we won't stop now to discuss railroading. Let's see what Joe has got for supper, for I'm hungry and I shouldn't be surprised if you were."

Indeed Rod was hungry, and just at that moment the word supper was the most welcome of the whole English language. First, though, he went to the wash-basin that he noticed at the forward end of the car. There he bathed his face and hands, brushed his hair, restored his clothing to something like order, and altogether made himself so presentable, that Conductor Tobin laughed when he saw him, and declared that he looked less like a stockman than ever.

How good that supper, taken from the mammoth lunch pails of the train crew, tasted, and what delicious coffee came steaming out of the smoke-blackened pot that Brakeman Joe lifted so carefully from the stove! To be sure it had to be taken without milk, but there was plenty of sugar, and when Rod passed his tin cup for a second helping, the coffee maker's face fairly beamed with gratified pride.

After these three and Smiler had finished their supper, Conductor Tobin lighted his pipe, and, climbing up into the cupola of the caboose, stretched himself comfortably on the cushioned seat arranged there for his especial accommodation. From here, through the windows ahead, behind, and on both sides of the cupola, he had an unobstructed view out into the night. Brakeman Joe went out over the tops of the cars to call in the other two brakeman of the train, and keep watch for them, while they went into the caboose and ate their supper. They looked curiously at Rod as they entered the car; but were too well used to seeing strangers riding there to ask any questions. They both spoke to Smiler though, and he wagged his tail as though recognizing old friends.

The dog could not go to them and jump up to be petted because Rod was attending to his wounds. He carefully bathed the cut under the left ear, from which considerable blood had flowed, and drew its edges together with some sticking plaster, of which he always carried a small quantity in his M. I. P. bag. Then, finding one of the dog's fore shoulders strained and swollen, he soaked it for some time in water as hot as the animal could bear. After arranging a comfortable bed in one corner of the car, he finally persuaded Smiler to lie there quietly, though not until he had submitted to a grateful licking of his face and hands.

Next the boy turned his attention to the supper dishes, and had them very nearly washed and wiped when Brakeman Joe returned, greatly to that stalwart fellow's surprise and delight; for Joe hated to wash dishes. By this time Rod had been nearly two hours on the train, and was so thoroughly tired that he concluded to lie down and rest until he should be wanted for something else. He did not mean to even close his eyes, but within three minutes he was fast asleep. All through the night he slept, while the long freight train, stopping only now and then for water, or to allow some faster train to pass it, rumbled heavily along toward the great city.

He could not at first realize where he was, when, in the gray of the next morning, a hand was laid on his shoulder, and Conductor Tobin's voice said: "Come, my young stockman, here we are at the end of our run, and it is time for you to be looking after your cattle." A quick dash of cold water on his head and face cleared the boy's faculties in an instant. Then Conductor Tobin pointed out the two stock cars full of cattle that were being uncoupled from the rest of the train, and bade him go with them to the stock-yard. There he was to see that the cattle were well watered and safely secured in the pen that would be assigned to them. Rod was also told that he might leave his bag in the caboose and come back, after he was through with his work, for a bit of breakfast with Brakeman Joe, who lived at the other end of the division, and always made the car his home when at this end. As for himself, Conductor Tobin said he must bid the boy good-by, as he lived a short distance out on the road, and must hurry to catch the train that would take him home. He would be back, ready to start out again with the through freight, that evening, and hoped Rod would come and tell him what luck he had in obtaining a position. Then rough but kind-hearted Conductor Tobin left the boy, never for a moment imagining that he was absolutely penniless and without friends in that part of the country, or in the great city across the river.

For the next two hours Rod worked hard and faithfully with the cattle committed to his charge, and then, anticipating with a keen appetite a share of Brakeman Joe's breakfast, he returned to where he had left the caboose. It was not there, nor could he find a trace of it. He saw plenty of other cabooses looking just like it, but none of them was the one he wanted.

He inquired of a busy switch-tender where it could be found, and the man asked him its number. He had not noticed. What was the number of the train with which it came in? Rod had no idea. The number of the locomotive that drew it then? The boy did not know that either.

"Well," said the man impatiently, "you don't seem to know much of anything, and I'd advise you to learn what it is you want to find out before you bother busy folks with questions."

So the poor fellow was left standing alone and bewildered in the great, busy freight-yard, friendless and hungry. He had lost even the few treasures contained in his M. I. P. bag, and never had life seemed darker or more hopeless. For some moments he could not think what to do, or which way to turn.

CHAPTER VIII.
EARNING A BREAKFAST.

If Rod Blake had only known the number of the caboose for which he was searching, he could easily have learned what had happened to it. Soon after he left it, while it was being switched on to a siding, one of its draw-bars became broken, and it had been sent to the repair shop, a mile or so away, to be put in condition for going out again that night. He had not thought of looking at its number, though; for he had yet to learn that on a railroad everything goes by numbers instead of by names. A few years ago all locomotives bore names, such as "Flying Cloud," "North Wind," etc., or were called after prominent men; but now they are simply numbered. It is the same with cars, except sleepers, drawing-rooms, and a few mail cars. Trains are also numbered, odd numbers being given to west or south bound, and even numbers to east or north bound trains. Thus, while a passenger says he is going out by the Chicago Limited, the Pacific Express, or the Fitchburg Local, the railroad man would say that he was going on No. 1, 3, or 5, as the case might be. The sections, from three to eight miles long, into which every road is divided, are numbered, as are all its bridges. Even the stations are numbered, and so are the tracks.

All this Rodman discovered afterwards; but he did not know it then, and so he was only bewildered by the switchman's questions. For a few minutes he stood irresolute, though keeping a sharp lookout for the hurrying switch engines, and moving cars that, singly or in trains, were flying in all directions about him, apparently without any reason or method. Finally he decided to follow out his original plan of going to the superintendent's office and asking for employment. By inquiry he found that it was located over the passenger station, nearly a mile away from where he stood. When he reached the station, and inquired for the person of whom he was in search, he was laughed at, and told that the "super" never came to his office at that time of day, nor until two or three hours later. So, feeling faint for want of breakfast, as well as tired and somewhat discouraged, the boy sat down in the great bustling waiting-room of the station.

At one side of the room was a lunch-counter, from which the odor of newly-made coffee was wafted to him in the most tantalizing manner. What wouldn't he give for a cup at that moment? But there was no use in thinking of such things; and so he resolutely turned his back upon the steaming urn, and the tempting pile of eatables by which it was surrounded. In watching the endless streams of passengers steadily ebbing and flowing past him, he almost forgot the emptiness of his stomach. Where could they all be going to, or coming from? Did people always travel in such overwhelming numbers, that it seemed as though the whole world were on the move, or was this some special occasion? He thought the latter must be the case, and wondered what the occasion was. Then there were the babies and children! How they swarmed about him! He soon found that he could keep pretty busy, and win many a grateful smile from anxious mothers, by capturing and picking up little toddlers who would persist in running about and falling down right in the way of hurrying passengers. He also kept an eye on the old ladies, who were so flustered and bewildered, and asked such meaningless questions of everybody, that he wondered how they were ever to reach their destinations in safety.

One of these deposited a perfect avalanche of little bags, packages, and umbrellas on the seat beside him. Several of them fell to the floor, and Rod was good-naturedly picking them up when he was startled by the sound of a clear, girlish voice that he knew as well as he knew his own, directly behind him. He turned, with a quickly beating heart, and saw Eltje Vanderveer. She was walking between her father and Snyder Appleby. They had already passed without seeing him, and had evidently just arrived by an early morning train from Euston.

Rod's first impulse was to run after them; and, starting to do so, he was only a step behind them when he heard Snyder say: "He must have money, because he refused a hundred dollars that the Major offered him. At any rate we'll hear from him soon enough if he gets hard up or into trouble. He isn't the kind of a----"

But Rod had already turned away, and what he wasn't, in Snyder's opinion, he never knew.

He had hardly resumed his seat, when there was a merry jingle on the floor beside him, and a quantity of silver coins began to roll in all directions. The nervous old lady of the bags and bundles had dropped her purse, and now she stood gazing at her scattered wealth, the very image of despair.

"Never mind, ma'am," said Rod, cheerily, as he began to capture the truant coins. "I'll have them all picked up in a moment." It took several minutes of searching here and there, under the seats, and in all sorts of out-of-the-way hiding places, before all the bits of silver were recovered, and handed to their owner.

She drew a great sigh of relief as she counted her money and found that none was lost. Then, beaming at the boy through her spectacles, she said: "Well, thee is an honest lad; and, if thee'll look after my bags while I get my ticket, and then help me to the train, I'll give thee a quarter."

Rod was on the point of saying, politely: "I shall be most happy to do anything I can for you, ma'am; but I couldn't think of accepting pay for it," when the thought of his position flashed over him. A quarter would buy him a breakfast, and it would be honorably earned too. Would it not be absolutely wrong to refuse it under the circumstances? Thus thinking, he touched his cap, and said: "Certainly I will do all I can to help you, ma'am, and will be glad of the chance to earn a quarter."

When the old lady had procured her ticket, and Rod had received the first bit of money he had ever earned in his life by helping her to a comfortable seat in the right car, she would have detained and questioned him, but for her fear that he might be carried off. So she bade him hurry from the car as quickly as possible, though it still lacked nearly ten minutes of the time of starting.

The hungry boy knew well enough where he wanted to go, and what he wanted to do, now. In about three seconds after leaving the car he was seated at the railroad lunch-counter, with a cup of coffee, two hard-boiled eggs, and a big hot roll before him. He could easily have disposed of twice as much; but prudently determined to save some of his money for another meal, which he realized, with a sigh, would be demanded by his vigorous appetite before the day was over.

To his dismay, when he asked the young woman behind the counter how much he owed for what he had eaten, she answered, "Twenty-five cents, please." He thought there must be some mistake, and asked her if there was not; but she answered: "Not at all. Ten cents for coffee, ten for eggs, and five for the roll." With this she swept Rod's solitary quarter into the money-drawer, and turned to wait on another customer.

"Well, it costs something to live," thought the boy, ruefully, as he walked away from the counter. "At that rate I could easily have eaten a dollar's worth of breakfast, and I certainly sha'n't choose this for my boarding place, whatever happens."

CHAPTER IX.
GAINING A FOOTHOLD.

Though he could have eaten more, Rod felt decidedly better for the meal so unexpectedly secured, and made up his mind that now was the time to see the superintendent and ask for employment. So he made his way to that gentleman's office, where he was met by a small boy, who told him that the superintendent had been there a few minutes before, but had gone away with President Vanderveer.

"When will he be back?" asked Rod.

"Not till he gets ready," was the reply; "but the best time to catch him is about five o'clock."

For the next six hours poor Rod wandered about the station and the railroad yard, with nothing to do and nobody to speak to, feeling about as lonely and uncomfortable as it is possible for a healthy and naturally light-hearted boy to feel. He strolled into the station twenty times to study the slow moving hands of its big clock, and never had the hours appeared to drag along so wearily. When not thus engaged he haunted the freight yard, mounting the steps of every caboose he saw, in the hope of recognizing it. At length, to his great joy, shortly before five o'clock he saw, through a window set in the door of one of these, the well-remembered interior in which he had spent the preceding night. He could not be mistaken, for there lay his own M. I. P. bag on one of the lockers. But the car was empty, and its doors were locked. Carefully observing its number, which was 18, and determined to return to it as quickly as possible, Rod directed his steps once more in the direction of the superintendent's office.

The same boy whom he had seen in the morning greeted him with an aggravating grin, and said: "You're too late. The 'super' was here half an hour ago; but he's left, and gone out over the road. Perhaps he won't be back for a week."

"Oh!" exclaimed Rod in such a hopeless tone that even the boy's stony young heart was touched by it.

"Is it R. R. B.?" he asked, meaning, "Are you on railroad business?"

"Yes," answered Rod, thinking his own initials were meant.

"Then perhaps the private secretary can attend to it," said the boy. "He's in there." Here he pointed with his thumb towards an inner room, "and I'll go see."

In a moment he returned, saying, "Yes. He says he'll see you if it's R. R. B., and you can go right in."

Rodman did as directed, and found himself in a handsomely-furnished office, which, somewhat to his surprise, was filled with cigarette smoke. In it, with his back turned toward the door, and apparently busily engaged in writing, a young man sat at one of the two desks that it contained.

"Well, sir," said this individual, without looking up, in a voice intended to be severe and business-like, but which was somewhat disguised by a cigarette held between his teeth, "What can I do for you?"

"I came," answered Rod, hesitatingly, "to see if the superintendent of this road could give me any employment on it."

The words were not out of his mouth, before the private secretary, wheeling abruptly about, disclosed the unwelcome face of Snyder Appleby.

"Well, if this isn't a pretty go!" he exclaimed, with a sneer. "So you've come here looking for work, have you? I'd like to know what you know about railroad business, anyhow? No, sir; you won't get a job on this road, not if I can help it, and I rather think I can. The best thing for you to do is to go back to Euston, and make up with the old gentleman. He's soft enough to forgive anything, if you're only humble enough. As for the idea of you trying to be a railroad man, it's simply absurd. We want men, not boys, in this business."

Too surprised and indignant to reply at once to this cruel speech, and fearful lest he should be unable to control his temper if he remained a moment longer in the room, Rodman turned, without a word, and hurried from it. He was choked with a bitter indignation, and could not breathe freely until he was once more outside the building, and in the busy railroad yard.

As he walked mechanically forward, hardly noting, in the raging tumult of his thoughts, whither his steps were tending, a heavy hand was laid on his shoulder, and a hearty voice exclaimed: "Hello, young fellow! Where have you been, and where are you bound? I've been looking for you everywhere. Here's your grip that

I was just taking to the lost-parcel room."

It was Brakeman Joe, with Rod's M. I. P. bag in his hand, and his honest, friendly countenance seemed to the unhappy boy the very most welcome face he had ever seen. They walked together to caboose Number 18, where Rod poured into the sympathizing ears of his railroad friend the story of his day's experience.

"Well, I'll be blowed!" exclaimed Brakeman Joe, using Conductor Tobin's favorite expression, when the boy had finished. "If that isn't tough luck, then I don't know what is. But I'll tell you what we'll do. I can't get you a place on the road, of course; but I believe you are just on time for a job, such as it is, that will put a few dollars in your pocket, and keep you for a day or two, besides giving you a chance to pick up some experience of a trainman's life."

"Oh, if you only will!----" began the boy, gratefully.

"Better wait till you hear what it is, and we see if we can get it," interrupted Joe. "You see the way of it is this, there was a gent around here awhile ago with a horse, that he wants to send out on our train, to some place in the western part of the State. I don't know just where it's going, but his brother is to meet it at the end of our run, and take charge of it from there. Now the chap that the gent had engaged to look after the horse that far, has gone back on him, and didn't show up here as he promised, and the man's looking for somebody else. We'll just go down to the stock-yard, and if he hasn't found anybody yet, maybe you can get the job. See?"

Half an hour later it was all arranged. The gentleman was found, and had not yet engaged any one to take the place of his missing man. He was so pleased with Rod's appearance, besides being so thoroughly satisfied by the flattering recommendations given him by Brakeman Joe, and the master of the stock-yard, who had noticed the boy in the morning, that he readily employed him, offering him five dollars for the trip.

So Rod's name was written on the way-bill, he helped get the horse, whose name was Juniper, comfortably fixed in the car set apart for him, and then he gladly accepted the gentleman's invitation to dine with him in a restaurant near by. There he received his final instructions.

CHAPTER X.
A THRILLING EXPERIENCE.

Between the time that Rod took charge of Juniper, and the time of the train's starting, the young "stockman," as he was termed on the way-bill, had some pretty lively experiences. Before the owner of the horse left, he handed the boy two dollars and fifty cents, which was half the amount he had agreed to pay him, and a note to his brother, requesting him to pay the bearer the same sum at the end of the trip. After spending fifty cents for a lunch, consisting of crackers, cheese, sandwiches, and a pie, for the boy had no idea of going hungry again if he could help it, nor of paying the extravagant prices charged at railroad lunch-counters, Rod took his place, with Juniper, in car number 1160, which was the one assigned to them. Here he proceeded to make the acquaintance of his charge; and, aided by a few lumps of sugar that he had obtained for this purpose, he soon succeeded in establishing the most friendly relations between them.

Suddenly, while he was patting and talking to the horse, car number 1160 received a heavy bump from a string of empties, that had just been sent flying down the track on which it stood, by a switch engine. Juniper was very nearly flung off his feet, and was greatly frightened. Before Rod could quiet him, there came another bump from the opposite direction, followed by a jerk. Then the car began to move, while Juniper, quivering in every limb, snorted with terror. Now came a period of "drilling," as it is called, that proved anything but pleasant either to the boy or to the frightened animal. The car was pushed and pulled from one track to another, sometimes alone and sometimes in company with other cars. The train of which it was to form a part was being made up, and the "drilling" was for the purpose of getting together the several cars bound to certain places, and of placing those that were to be dropped off first, behind those that were to make the longest runs.

Juniper's fears increased with each moment, until at length, when a passenger locomotive, with shrieking whistle, rushed past within a few feet, he gave a jump that broke the rope halter confining him, and bounded to the extreme end of the car. Rod sprang to the open door--not with any idea of leaving the car, oh, no! his sense of duty was too strong for that, but for the purpose of closing it so that the horse should not leap out. Then he approached the terrified animal with soothing words, and caught hold of the broken halter. At the same moment the car was again set in motion, and the horse, now wild with terror, flew to the other end, dragging Rod after him. The only lantern in the car was overturned and its light extinguished, so that the struggle between boy and horse was continued in utter darkness. Finally a tremendous bump of the car flung the horse to the floor; and, before he could regain his feet, Rod was sitting on his head. The boy was panting from his exertions, as well as bruised from head to foot; but he was thankful to feel that no bones were broken, and hoped the horse had escaped serious injury as well as himself.

After several minutes of quiet he became satisfied that that last bump was the end of the drilling, and that car number 1160 had at length reached its assigned position in the train. Still he did not think it safe to let the horse up just yet, and so he waited until he heard voices outside. Then he called for help. The next moment the car door was pushed open, and Conductor Tobin, followed by Brakeman Joe, entered it.

"Well, I'll be everlastingly blowed!" cried Conductor Tobin, using the very strongest form of his peculiar expression, as the light from his lantern fell on the strange tableau presented by the boy and horse. "If this doesn't beat all the stock-tending I ever heard of. Joe here was just telling me you was going out with us to-night, in charge of a horse, and we were looking for your car. But what are you doing to him?"

"Sitting on his head," answered Rod, gravely.

"So I see," said Conductor Tobin, "and you look very comfortable; but how does he like it?"

"I don't suppose he likes it at all," replied the boy; "but I couldn't think of anything else to do." Then he told them of the terror inspired in the animal by the recent drilling; how it had broken loose and dragged him up and down the car, and how he came to occupy his present position.

"Well, you've got sand!" remarked Conductor Tobin admiringly when the story was finished. "More 'n I have," he added. "I wouldn't have stayed here in the dark, with a loose horse tearing round like mad. Not for a month's pay I wouldn't."

"No more would I," said Brakeman Joe; "a scared hoss is a terror."

Then they brought some stout ropes, and Juniper was helped to his feet, securely fastened and soothed and petted until all his recent terror was forgotten. To Rod's great delight he was found to be uninjured, except for some insignificant scratches; and by his recent experience he was so well broken to railroad riding that he endured the long trip that followed with the utmost composure.

CHAPTER XI.
A BATTLE WITH TRAMPS.

After quieting Juniper, and having the satisfaction of seeing him begin to eat hay quite as though he were in his own stable, Rod left the car and followed his railroad friends in order to learn something about getting a train ready for its run. He found them walking on opposite sides of it, examining each car by the light of their lanterns, and calling to each other the inscriptions on the little leaden seals by which the doors were fastened. These told where the cars came from, which information, together with the car numbers, and the initials showing to what road they belonged, Conductor Tobin jotted down in his train-book. He also compared it with similar information noted on certain brown cards, about as wide and twice as long as ordinary playing-cards, a package of which he carried in his hand. The destinations of the several cars could also be learned from these cards, which are called "running slips." Each car in the train was represented by one of them, which would accompany it wherever it went, being handed from one conductor to another, until its final destination was reached.

At length, about ten o'clock, through Freight Number 73, to which car number 1160 was attached, received its "clearance," or order to start, from the train-dispatcher, and began to move heavily out from the yard, on to the main west-bound track. Juniper now did not seem to mind the motion of the car in the least; but continued quietly eating his hay as though he had been a railroad traveller all his life. So Rod, who had watched him a little anxiously at first, had nothing to do but stand at the open door of his car and gaze at what scenery the darkness disclosed. Now that he was beginning to comprehend their use, he was deeply interested in the bright red, green, and white lights of the semaphore signals that guarded every switch and siding. He knew that at night a white light displayed from the top of a post, or swung across the track in the form of a lantern, meant safety, a red light meant danger, and a green light meant caution. If it had been daytime he would have seen thin wooden blades, about four feet long by six inches wide, pivoted near the top of the same posts that now displayed the lights. He would have learned that when these stretched out horizontally over the track, their warning colors must be regarded by every engineman; while if they hung down at an angle, no attention need be paid to them.

Being a very observant boy, as well as keenly interested in everything to be seen on a railroad, Rod soon discovered that the semaphore lights also appeared at intervals of a few miles along the track, at places where there were no switches, and that these always moved as soon as the train passed them. He afterwards discovered that these guarded the ends of the five-mile blocks, into which the road was divided along its entire length. Each of the stations, at these points, is occupied by a telegraph operator who, as soon as the train enters his block, displays a red danger signal behind it. This forbids any other train to enter the block, on that track, until he receives word from the operator at the other end of the block that the first train has passed out of it. Then he changes his signal from red to white, as a notice that the block is free for the admission of the next train. This "block system," as it is called, which is now in use on all principal railroad lines, renders travel over them very much safer than it used to be before the system was devised.

After watching the semaphore lights for some time, and after assuring himself that Juniper was riding comfortably, Rod spread a blanket, that Brakeman Joe had loaned him, over a pile of loose hay, placed his M. I. P. bag for a pillow, and in a few minutes was sleeping on this rude bed as soundly as though he were at home.

Some hours later the long, heavily laden train stopped at the foot of the steep grade just east of Euston, and was cut in two in order that half of it might be drawn to the top at a time. Rear Brakeman Joe was left to guard the part of the train that remained behind, and he did this by walking back a few hundred yards along the track, and placing a torpedo on top of one of the rails. Then he went back as much farther and placed two torpedoes, one a rail's length behind the other.

These railroad torpedoes are small, round tin boxes, about the size of a silver dollar, filled with percussion powder. To each is attached two little straps of lead, which are bent under the upper part of the rail to hold the torpedo in position. When it is struck by the ponderous wheels of a locomotive, it explodes with the sound of a cannon cracker. The explosion of two torpedoes, one directly after the other, is the signal for caution, and bids the engineman proceed slowly, keeping a sharp lookout for danger. The explosion of a single torpedo is the signal of immediate danger, and bids him stop his train as quickly as possible. Thus Brakeman Joe had protected his train by arranging a cautionary signal, which would be followed immediately by that of danger. Before his train started again he intended to take up the single torpedo, leaving only those calling for caution, to show that the freight had been delayed. In the meantime he decided to walk back to the cars left in his charge and see that no one was meddling with them.

Rod was too soundly asleep to know anything of all this, nor did he know when an ugly-looking fellow peered cautiously into his car, and said, in a low tone: "This here ain't it. It must be the one ahead." The first thing of which he was conscious was hearing, as in a dream, the sound of blows, mingled with shouts, and a pistol shot, and then Brakeman Joe's voice calling: "Rod! Rod Blake! Help! quick!"

An instant later the boy had leaped from the car, and was by his friend's side, engaged in a desperate struggle with four as villainous-looking tramps as could well be found; though, of course, he could not judge of their appearance in the darkness. Joe was wielding the heavy oak stick that at other times he used as a lever to aid him in twisting the brake wheels; but Rod was obliged to depend entirely on his fists. The skill with which he used these was evidently a surprise to the big fellow who rushed at him, only to receive a stinging blow in the face, which was followed by others delivered with equal promptness and effect. There were a few minutes of fierce but confused fighting. Then, all at once, Rod found himself standing alone beside a car the door of which was half-way open. Two of the tramps had mysteriously disappeared; he himself had sent a third staggering backward down the bank into a clump of bushes, and he could hear Brakeman Joe chasing the fourth down the track.

A few minutes later the locomotive came back, sounding four long blasts and one short one on its whistle, as a recall signal for the rear flagman. It was coupled on, and some one waved a lantern, with an up-and-down motion, from the rear of the train, as a signal to go ahead. The engineman opened the throttle, and the great driving wheels spun round furiously; but the train refused to move. He sounded two long whistle blasts as a signal to throw off brakes. Then a lantern was seen moving over the tops of the cars, the brakes that had been holding them, were loosened, and the signal to go ahead was again waved. After this the lantern disappeared as though it had been taken into the caboose, and the train moved on.

Its severed parts were re-united at the top of the grade, and it passed on out of the block in which all these events had taken place, before Conductor Tobin, who had wondered somewhat at not seeing Brakeman Joe, discovered that the faithful fellow was missing. He was not on top of any of the cars, nor in the caboose, and must have been left behind. Well, it was too late to stop for him now. Freight Number 73 must side-track at the next station, to allow the night express to pass, and it had already been so delayed, that there was no time to lose.

When the station was reached, and Conductor Tobin had seen his train safely side-tracked, he went to look for Rod Blake. He meant to ask the boy to take Brakeman Joe's place for the rest of the run, or until that individual should rejoin them by coming ahead on some faster train. To his surprise the young stockman was not in car number 1160, nor could a trace of him be found. He, too, had disappeared and the conductor began to feel somewhat alarmed, as well as puzzled, by such a curious and unaccountable state of affairs.

CHAPTER XII.
BOUND, GAGGED, AND A PRISONER.

When Rod Blake was left standing alone beside the train, after the short but sharp encounter with tramps described in the preceding chapter, he was as bewildered by its sudden termination as he had been, on awaking from a sound sleep, to find himself engaged in it. He knew what had become of two of the tramps, for one of them he had sent staggering backward down the embankment, and Brakeman Joe was at that moment pursuing the second; but the disappearance of the others was a mystery. What could have become of them? They must have slipped away unnoticed, and taken advantage of the darkness to make good their escape. "Yes, that must be it; for tramps are always cowards," thought the boy. "But four of them ought to have whipped two of us easy enough."

Then he wondered what the object of the attack could have been, and what the tramps were after. All at once it flashed into his mind that the M. S. and T. car number 50, beside which he was standing, was filled with costly silks and laces from France which were being sent West in bond. He had overheard Conductor Tobin say so; and, now, there was the door of that very car half-way open. The tramps must have learned of its valuable contents in some way, and been attempting to rob it when Brakeman Joe discovered them. What a plucky fellow Joe was to tackle them single-handed.

"I wonder if they got anything before he caught them?" thought the boy; and, to satisfy his curiosity on this point, he went to his own car for the lantern that was still hanging in it, and returned to car number 50, determined to have a look at its interior. As he could not see much of it from the ground, he set the lantern just within the open doorway, and began to climb in after it. He had hardly stepped inside, and was stooping to pick up his lantern, when he was knocked down by a heavy blow, and immediately seized by two men who sprang from out of the darkness on either side of him. Without a word they bound his wrists with a stout bit of cord, and, thrusting his own handkerchief into his mouth, fastened it securely so that he could not utter a sound. Then they allowed him to rise and sit on a box, where they took the precaution of passing a rope about his body and making it fast to an iron stanchion near the door.

Having thus secured him, one of the men, holding the lantern close to the boy's face, said in a threatening tone: "Now, my chicken, perhaps this'll be a lesson to you never to interfere again in a business that doesn't concern you."

"Hello!" exclaimed the other, as he recognized Rod's features, "if this ere hain't the same cove wot set the dog onto me last night. Oh, you young willin, I'll get even with you now!"

With this he made a motion as though to strike the helpless prisoner; but the other tramp restrained him, saying: "Hold on, Bill, we hain't got no time for fooling now. Don't you hear the engine coming back? I'll take this lantern and give 'em the signal to go ahead, in case that fool of a brakeman doesn't turn up on time, which I don't believe he will." Here the fellow chuckled meaningly. "You," he continued, "want to stay right here, and begin to pitch out the boxes as soon as she starts, and the rest of us'll be on hand to gather 'em in. You can easy jump out when she slows up at the top of the grade. You want to be sure, though, and shut the door behind you so as nothing won't be suspected, and so this chap'll have a good, long ride undisturbed by visitors; see?"

If Rod could not talk, he could still hear; and, by paying close attention to this conversation, he formed a very clear idea of the tramps' plans. They meant to rob car number 50 of as many of its valuable packages as Bill could throw from it while the train was on the grade. He felt satisfied that they had, in some way, disposed of Brakeman Joe. Now, they intended to get rid of him by leaving him in the closed car, helplessly bound, and unable to call for assistance. What would become of him? That car might be going to San Francisco for aught he knew, and its door might not be opened for days, or even weeks. It might not be opened until he was dead of thirst or starvation. What tortures might he not suffer in this moving prison? It seemed as though these thoughts would drive him crazy, and he realized that if he wished to retain his senses and think out a way of escape, he must not dwell upon them.

So he tried to think of plans for outwitting the tramps. The chances of so doing seemed slender enough; but he felt certain there must be some way. In the meantime one of his assailants had left the car, very nearly closing the door as he did so for fear lest somebody might come along and notice it if it were wide open. He had taken the lantern with him, the train was in motion, the young tramp called Bill was already preparing to carry out his part of the programme and begin throwing out the boxes. Suddenly, like a flash of lightning, a plan that would not only save the car from being robbed, but would ensure its door being opened before he could die of either thirst or hunger, darted into Rod's mind.

He knew that the car door closed with a spring latch that could only be opened from the outside. He knew that no one could board the train, now that it was in motion, to open the door. Above all he knew that if the young tramp were shut in there with him he would not suffer long from hunger and thirst before raising his voice and making his presence known to outsiders. Rod could reach the door with his foot. A quick push, the welcome click of the latch as it sprang sharply into place, and the plan was carried out.

It took Bill, the young tramp, several minutes to find out what had happened, and that the door could not be opened from the inside. When he finally realized his position he broke out with a torrent of yells and threats against his recent companions. It never occurred to him that Rod had closed the door. He imagined that it must have been done from the outside, by one of his fellow thieves, and his rage against them knew no bounds. If he had for a moment suspected the captive, whom he regarded as helplessly bound, he would undoubtedly have directed his fury towards him, and Rod might have suffered severely at his hands. As it was, he only yelled and kicked against the door until the train began to slow up at the top of the grade. Then, fearful of attracting undesirable attention, he subsided into a sullen silence.

While these things were happening to Rod, Brakeman Joe was suffering even greater misfortunes. His left arm had been broken by the pistol shot, that was one of the first sounds of the fight by which the young stockman was awakened; and when he started in pursuit of the flying tramp, he was weaker than he realized, from loss of blood. The tramp quickly discovered that he could easily keep out of his pursuer's way. Judging from this that the Brakeman must be either wounded or exhausted, he gradually slackened his pace, until Joe was close upon him. Then springing to one side, and whirling around, the tramp dealt the poor fellow a blow on the head with the butt of a revolver, that stretched him senseless across the rails of the west-bound track. After satisfying himself that his victim was not in a condition to molest him again for some time to come, and brutally leaving him where he had fallen, directly in the path of the next west-bound train, the tramp began leisurely to retrace his steps toward Freight Number 73, in the plunder of which he now hoped to take a part.

CHAPTER XIII.
HOW BRAKEMAN JOE WAS SAVED.

For ten minutes Brakeman Joe lies insensible and motionless, just as he fell. His own train has gone on without him, and now another is approaching. Its shrill whistle sounds near at hand, and the rails, across which the helpless form is stretched, are already quivering with the thrill of its coming. There seems no earthly help for him; nothing to warn the controlling mind of that on-rushing mass of his presence. In a few seconds the tragedy will be over.

Suddenly, crack! crack! two loud reports ring out sharply above the roar and rattle of the train, one just after the other. The engineman is keenly alert on the instant; and, with one hand on the brake lever, the other on the throttle, he peers steadily ahead. The head-light, that seems so dazzling, and to cast its radiance so far, to those approaching it, in reality illumines but a short space to him who sits behind it, and the engineman sees no evidence of danger. There is no red beacon to stop him, nor any train on the track ahead. He is beginning to think the alarm a false one, when another report, loud and imperative, rings in his startled ear. In an instant the powerful air brakes are grinding against the wheels of every car in the night express, until the track is lighted with a blaze of streaming sparks. A moment later the rushing train is brought to a stop, inside half its own length.

Even now nobody knew why it had been stopped, nor what danger threatened it. It was not until the engineman left his cab, and discovered the senseless form of Brakeman Joe lying across the rails, less than a hundred feet away, that he knew why he had been signalled. The wounded man was recognized at once, as belonging to the train ahead of them; but how he came in that sad plight, and who had placed the warning torpedoes to which he owed his escape from death, were perplexing questions that none could answer.

Very tenderly they lifted him, and laid him in the baggage car. Here Conductor Tobin found him a few minutes later, when, to his surprise, the night express, that generally whirled past him at full speed, slowed up and halted beside his own train, standing on the siding. "Yes," this was his brakeman, one of the best and most faithful fellows in the service; but how he got where they found him, or what had happened, he could not explain. He had lost another man off his train that night, a young fellow named Rodman Blake. Had they seen anything of him? "No! well, then he must have thrown up his job and gone into Euston where he belonged. Good-night." In another minute only a far-away murmur among the sleeping hills told of the passing of the night express.

Brakeman Joe was placed on the station agent's little cot bed, and the doctor was sent for. That was all they could do, and so Freight Number 73 also pulled out, leaving him behind. A minute later, and it too was gone, and the drowsy echoes answered its heavy rumblings faintly and more faintly, until they again fell asleep, and all was still.

Through the long hours of the night Rod Blake sat and silently suffered. The distress of the gag in his mouth became wellnigh intolerable, and his wrists swelled beneath the cords that bound them, until he could have cried out with the pain. He grew thirsty too. Oh, so thirsty! and it seemed as though the daylight would never come. He had no idea what good, or even what change for the better, the daylight would bring him; but still he longed for it. Nor was the young tramp who shared his imprisonment at all happy or comfortable. He too was thirsty, and hungry as well, and though he was not gagged nor bound, he suffered, in anticipation, the punishment he expected to receive when he and his wickedness should be discovered. Thus, whenever the train stopped, a sense of his just deserts terrified him into silence; though while it was in motion his ravings were terrible to hear.

At length the morning light began to show itself through chinks and crevices of the closed car. Conductor Tobin and his men reached the end of their run, and turned the train over to a new crew, who brought with them a fresh locomotive and their own caboose.

Still the young tramp would not give in. The morning was nearly gone, and Rod was desperate with suffering, before he did, and, during a stop, began to shout to be let out. Nobody heard him, apparently, and when the train again moved on, the situation of the prisoners was as bad as ever.

Now the fellow began to grow as much alarmed for fear he would not be discovered, as he had previously been for fear lest he should be. In this state of mind he decided that at the next stop the shouting for help should be undertaken by two voices instead of one. So he removed the gag from Rod's mouth, and cut the cord by which his wrists were bound. The poor lad's throat was dry and husky; but he readily agreed to aid in raising a shout, as soon as the train should stop.

In the meantime the arrival of Freight Number 73 was awaited with a lively interest at the very station it was approaching, when this agreement between the prisoners was made. It was aroused by a despatch, just sent along the line by the agent in whose charge Brakeman Joe had been left. The despatch stated that he had recovered sufficiently to give a partial account of what had been done to him by a gang of thieves, whom he had discovered trying to rob car number 50. It requested the first agent who should see Train Number 73, to examine into the condition of car number 50, and discover if anything had been stolen from it. It also stated that Brakeman Joe was very anxious concerning the safety of a young stockman, who had been on the train, and assisted him to drive off the thieves; but who had not since been heard from.

Thus, while the imprisoned inmates of car number 50 were waiting with feverish impatience for the train to reach a station at which it would stop, the railroad men belonging to this station, were waiting for it with a lively curiosity, that was wholly centered on car number 50.

CHAPTER XIV.
THE SUPERINTENDENT INVESTIGATES.

At length a long-drawn whistle from the locomotive attached to Freight Number 73, warned Rod and his fellow-prisoner that the time for them to make a combined effort for liberty was at hand. It also notified the curious watchers at the station of the approach of the train for which they were waiting. The trainmen were surprised at the unusual number of people gathered about the station, and the evident interest with which their arrival was regarded. At the same time those composing the little throng of waiting spectators were amazed, as the train drew up and stopped, to hear loud cries for help proceeding from a car in its centre.

"It's number 50!" exclaimed one, "the very car we are looking for."

"So it is! Break open the door! Some one is being murdered in there!" shouted other voices, and a rush was made for the car.

As its door was pushed open, by a dozen eager hands, a wretched-looked figure, who had evidently been pressing closely against it, and was unprepared for such a sudden movement, pitched out headlong into the crowd. As he staggered to his feet he tried to force his way through them, with the evident intention of running away; but he was seized and held.

For a moment the whole attention of the spectators was directed toward him, and he was stupefied by the multitude of questions showered upon him at once. Then some one cried "Look out! There's another in there!" and immediately poor

Rod was roughly dragged to the ground. "Take them into the waiting-room, and see that they don't escape while I examine the car. There may be more of the gang hidden in there," commanded the station agent. So to the waiting-room the prisoners were hustled with scant ceremony. As yet no one knew what they had done, nor even what they were charged with doing; but every one agreed that they were two of the toughest looking young villains ever seen in that part of the country.

During the confusion, no one had paid any attention to the arrival, from the west, of a locomotive drawing a single car. Nor did they notice a brisk, business-like appearing man who left this car, and walked, with a quick step, toward the waiting-room. Every one therefore looked up in surprise when he entered it and demanded, in a tone of authority, "What's the trouble here?"

Instantly a murmur was heard of, "It's the superintendent. It's the 'super' himself"; and, as the crowd respectfully made way for him, a dozen of voices were raised in attempted explanation of what had happened. As no one really knew what had happened, no two of the voices told the same story; but the superintendent catching the words "murderers, thieves, tramps, brakeman killed, and car robbed," became convinced that he had a most serious case on his hands, and that the disreputable-looking young fellows before him must be exceedingly dangerous characters. In order to arrive at an understanding of the case more quickly, he ordered the room to be cleared of all except the prisoners, the station agent, and the trainmen of Freight Number 73, whom he told to guard the doors.

He first examined the conductor, who was as surprised as any one else to find that he had been carrying two passengers of whom he knew nothing on his train. He had no information to give, excepting what Conductor Tobin had told him, and what the superintendent had already learned by telegraph, of Brakeman Joe's condition. The other trainmen knew nothing more.

The station agent told of the despatch he had received, of the finding of the lads in car number 50, and that its contents were apparently untouched.

Here the superintendent dismissed the trainmen, and ordered Freight Number 73 to go ahead. Then, with new guards stationed at the doors, he proceeded to question the prisoners themselves. As Bill, the tramp, seemed to be the elder of the two, he was the first examined. In answer to the questions who he was, where he came from, and what he had been doing in car number 50, Bill said, with exactly the manner he would have used in addressing a Police Justice:

"Please yer Honor we's pards, me an' him is, an' we's bin tendin' stock on de road. We was on de train last night when it was attackeded by a lot of fellers who was beatin' de brakeman. We went to help him, an' was chucked inter de car, an' de door locked on us. We's bin tryin' to get out even since, me an' him has, yer Honor, but we couldn't make nobody hear us till we got here. We's nearly dead for food an' drink, yer Honor, an' we's honest, hard-working boys, an' dat's de truth if I die for it, yer Honor. He'd tell yer de same, but fer a bit of a difference me and him had when he swore to git even wid me. So maybe he'll lie now; but yer Honor can depend on what I'm--"

"That will do," interrupted the superintendent. Then turning to Rodman he asked, "What have you to say for yourself?"

"If you'll please give me a drink of water I'll try to tell all I know of this affair," answered the boy huskily, now speaking for the first time since he had been taken from the car.

When the water was brought, and Bill had been given a drink as well as himself, Rod continued, "I was a stockman on that train in charge of a horse"--

"Jest as I was a-tellin' yer Honor," murmured Bill.

"And there was a fight with tramps, who attempted to rob the car in which we were found."

Here Bill nodded his head approvingly as much as to say "I told you so."

"But this fellow was one of them, and he helped make a prisoner of me, and to bind and gag me. He would have thrown the freight out of the car to those who were waiting outside to receive it, if I hadn't succeeded in closing the door, and locking us both in--"

"Ooo! didn't I tell yer Honor he'd maybe lie on me?" protested Bill.

"Keep quiet!" commanded the superintendent sharply, and then to Rod he said: "How can you prove your statements?"

"I can prove that I was bound and gagged by these marks," replied the boy, pointing to the sides of his mouth which were red and chafed, and holding out his swollen wrists for the superintendent's inspection. "And I can prove that I was travelling in charge of a horse by this." Here Rod produced the note from Juniper's owner, asking his brother to pay the bearer two dollars and a half upon the safe delivery of the horse.

"I have a paper too," broke in Bill, fumbling in his pockets. From one of them he finally produced a dirty note, signed by a Western cattle dealer, and authorizing one Bill Miner to take charge of certain stock about to be shipped over the New York and Western railroad.

The superintendent read the two notes, and looked at the two young fellows. In general appearance one was very nearly as bad as the other; for, though Rod did not realize the fact, his clothing and person were so torn and dirty from the fight of the preceding night and his subsequent rough experience, that he looked very nearly as much of a tramp as Bill himself.

"I wonder which of you I am to believe, or if either is telling me the truth?" said the superintendent dubiously, half aloud and half to himself.

CHAPTER XV.
SMILER TO THE RESCUE.

At that moment a small dog walked into the room, wagging his tail with an air of being perfectly at home there. Rod was the first to notice him, and his eye lighted with a gleam of genuine pleasure.

"Smiler? Smiler, old dog!" he said.

The next instant Smiler was licking his face and testifying to his joy at again meeting this friend, in the most extravagant manner. Suddenly he caught sight of Bill, and drawing back his upper lip with an ominous growl, would have flown at the young tramp had not Rodman restrained him.

"That settles it, so far as I am concerned," exclaimed the superintendent, with a relieved air. "Any one that Smiler recognizes as a friend must be an honest fellow; while the person whom Smiler calls an enemy, must have given him good cause for his enmity, and is to be regarded with distrust by all railroad men. Now, I am going to carry you two chaps to the Junction where Conductor Tobin and his crew are lying off to-day. There, I have no doubt, this whole matter will be explained satisfactorily to me and to one of you, as well as with perfect justice to you both."

Smiler, who had reached this station on a passenger locomotive, now attached himself resolutely to Rod, and followed him into the superintendent's private car, here he was made as cordially welcome as he would have been in the humblest caboose on the road. Some of his enthusiastic admirers declared that Smiler owned the road; while all admitted that there was but one other individual connected with it, whose appearance was so uniformly welcome as his, and that was the paymaster.

Now, there was a marked difference shown between the treatment of Smiler's friend, and that of his enemy. The former was invited to sit down with the superintendent and eat dinner, which was announced as ready soon after they left the station; but Bill was consigned to the care of a brakeman who received strict orders not to give him a chance to escape. He was given a substantial meal of course; for Mr. Hill the superintendent was not a man who would permit anybody to suffer from hunger if he could help it. Here the courtesy extended to him ended, and he was treated in all respects like a prisoner. Most of the time he rode in sullen silence; but occasionally he broke forth with vehement protestations of his innocence, and of the truth of the story he had told.

Rodman, on the other hand, was treated with marked consideration; for, not only was he a friend of Smiler's, but the more Mr. Hill talked with him the more he believed him to be a gentleman, as well as an honest, truth-telling lad, who had, by a brave and prompt action, saved the railroad company a large amount of property. He was confirmed in his belief that Rod was a gentleman, by his having asked to be allowed to wash his face and hands before sitting down to dinner. The lad was shocked at his own appearance when he glanced into a mirror, and the superintendent smiled at the wonderful change made by the use of soap, water, and brushes, when he emerged from the well-appointed dressing-room of the car.

While they sat at table Mr. Hill drew the lad's story from him, including the manner in which he had obtained Smiler's friendship, and his desire to become a railroad man. Rod did not however mention the name of President Vanderveer; for he was desirous of winning success by himself, and on his own merits, nor did he give his reasons for leaving Euston.

When the locomotive, drawing the superintendent's private car, and displaying two white flags in front to denote that it was running as an "extra" train, drew up, a couple of hours later, at the Junction, Rod was asked to remain in the car for a few minutes, and Bill was ordered to do so. Then Mr. Hill walked over to caboose

number 18, in which, as he expected, he found Conductor Tobin and his two brakemen fast asleep, with bits of mosquito netting spread over their faces to keep off the
flies. Conductor Tobin was greatly confused when he discovered who was shaking
him into wakefulness, and began to apologize for having been asleep.

"No excuses are necessary, Tobin," said the other kindly. "A man who works as
faithfully as you do at night, has a perfect right to sleep in the daytime. I wouldn't
have disturbed you, but that I wanted to ask if you were acquainted with a young
fellow named Rod Blake."

Yes, indeed! Conductor Tobin not only knew the lad, but was, at that moment, quite anxious concerning him. He had learned by telegraph from Brakeman
Joe, further particulars of the occurrences of the preceding night, including Rod's
splendid behavior during the fight with the would-be thieves. Since then nothing
had been heard from him, and the conductor greatly feared that the brave young
fellow had met with some harm.

"Do you consider him a person whose word is to be trusted?" asked the superintendent.

"Well, sir," answered Conductor Tobin, "I haven't known him long, seeing that
I first met him only night before last; but I've already seen enough of him to be willing to take his word as quick as that of any man living."

"That is saying a good deal," laughed the superintendent, "but I believe you are
right. If I am any judge of character, that lad is an honest fellow." Then he explained
how, and under what circumstances he had met Rod, and ending by asking, "What
sort of a railroad man do you think he would make?"

"First-rate, sir! He seems to me to be one who knows when he is wanted, and
who always turns up at the right time."

"Then you wouldn't mind having him on your train, while Joe is laid by?"

"I should be proud to have him, sir, and to be the one to start him on the right
track as a railroader."

"Very well, we will consider it settled, then, and I will send him over to you. I
want you to do the best you can by him, and remember that from this time on I take
a personal interest in his welfare, though of course you needn't tell him so."

Rod was more than delighted when Mr. Hill returned to the car, and offered
him the position of brakeman on Conductor Tobin's train. He promptly and gladly

accepted it, and tried to thank the superintendent for giving it to him; but that gentleman said: "Never mind expressing any thanks in words. Express them by deeds instead, and remember, that you can win a certain success in railroad life, by keeping on as you have begun and by always being on time."

Thus Rod secured a position; a humble one to be sure, but one that he had sought and won wholly by merit. When Snyder Appleby heard of it he was filled with jealous anger. He declared that there was not room for both of them on that road, even if one was only a brakeman, and vowed that if he could manage it, his adopted cousin should find it harder to keep his position than it had been to win it.

CHAPTER XVI.
SNYDER APPLEBY'S JEALOUSY.

Bill Miner, the tramp, underwent some novel mental experiences on the day that Rod obtained his position. In the first place the young fellow, whom he had treated so badly, came to him while the superintendent was interviewing Conductor Tobin, and said:

"Look here, Bill, you and I suffered a good deal together last night, and you know it was mostly your fault that we did so; but I'll forgive you for my share of the suffering if you'll only confess the whole business to the superintendent. He is bound to find out all about it anyway; for he finds out everything; but he'll think a good deal more of you if you own up like a man. I would like to be your friend; but my friends must be honest fellows, who are willing to work for a living, not tramps and thieves. Now shake hands, and make up your mind to do what I have asked you."

Mr. Hill's return interrupted the conversation at this point; but it left Bill in an unusually reflective state of mind. No gentleman, such as his late companion in captivity evidently was, had ever shaken hands with, or asked a favor of him before. In all his hard young life no one had ever proposed that he should try honesty and hard work. Ever since he could remember anything, his associates had advised dishonesty, and the shirking of work in every possible way. Yet, now that he thought of it, he had worked hard, all his life, at being dishonest. Now what had he to show for it? Nothing but rags, and poverty, and a bad reputation. He wondered how it would seem to be honest, and do honest work, and associate only with honest people. He had half a mind to try it, just out of curiosity. The idea of he, Bill the tramp, being an honest workman, and perhaps, even getting to be called "Honest Bill," struck him as so odd that he chuckled hoarsely over it.

"What are you laughing at?" demanded the brakeman who stood on the rear platform of the car to prevent his escape, and who looked suspiciously in at the door to discover the meaning of this novel sound from his prisoner.

"Nothing," replied Bill.

"Well, I wish I could get so much fun out of nothing as you seem able to," said the brakeman, who was particularly down on tramps. "I reckon the super'll give you something to laugh about directly that won't seem so funny," he added significantly.

But Bill did not mind this. He was too busy with his own thoughts. Besides he was used to such speeches, and was also listening to something else just at that moment. He was listening to the conversation between Rod and the superintendent. It certainly was a fine thing for a boy to be talked to as the greatest man he had ever known was now talking to his one honest friend, and to be offered such a position too. How he would like to be a brakeman; and, if he were one, how well he would know how to deal with tramps. He wondered what Mr. Hill meant by being "on time." Perhaps it meant being honest.

Then Rod left the car, giving him a nod and a smile as he did so. A moment later it was again whirling away toward New York, and the superintendent, coming to where the young tramp was sitting, said: "Now, sir, I'm ready to attend to your case. Are you willing to tell me what you know about this business of robbing our freight trains? Or do you prefer to stick to your lying story and go to prison for it?"

"I'll tell you all I know, if you'll give me a job for it," answered Bill, with a sudden resolution to try for Rod Blake's friendship, and at the same time to make a good bargain for himself if he could.

Regarding him keenly, the superintendent said: "So you want to be paid for being honest, do you? Well, I don't know but what you are right. Honesty is well worth paying for. So, if you will tell me, truthfully, all you know of this business I promise you a job that will earn you an honest living, and that you can keep just so long as you work faithfully at it."

"Honesty again. How often these gentlemen use the word, and how much they seem to think of it," thought Bill. However, as it seemed to promise something different from anything he had ever known, he determined to try it, and see what it would do for him. So he told, in his awkward fashion, all that he knew of the gang of tramp thieves, who had been for some time systematically robbing freight trains at several points along the road, and Mr. Hill listened to him with the deepest interest.

As a speedy result of this confession a freight clerk in the main office of the company, who had been giving secret information to the thieves, was discharged the very next day. Brown, the chief of the company's detectives, learned where and how he could discover the places where the stolen goods were hidden, and was thus enabled to recover a large portion of them. And Bill Miner, no longer Bill the tramp, found himself doing honest work, as a locomotive wiper and assistant hostler, in a round house, at a salary of one dollar and twenty-nine cents per day.

Certainly Rod Blake's influence was being felt on the New York and Western railroad.

After his conversation with Bill, the busy superintendent found time to stop his flying car at the station where Brakeman Joe lay suffering from his wounds, to speak a few kindly words to the faithful fellow, praise his bravery, and assure him that his full pay should be continued until he had entirely recovered from his injuries and was able to resume duty.

Late that afternoon the private car finished its long journey in the station at the terminus of the road, and Mr. Hill hastened to his own office. The moment he opened the door of the inner room a cloud of cigarette smoke issued from it, and a frown settled on his face as he hesitated a moment on the threshold. His private secretary, who had been comfortably tilted back in the superintendent's own easy chair, puffing wreathes of smoke from a cigarette, started to his feet. "We did not expect you to return so soon, sir"--he began.

"Evidently not," interrupted Mr. Hill dryly; "You are the young man recommended to me by President Vanderveer, I believe?"

"Yes, sir."

"Well, sir, you will please to remember for the future, that neither in this office, nor in any other belonging to the company, is cigarette smoking among the qualifications required of our employees. If you must smoke during business hours, I will endeavor to fill your position with somebody who is not under that necessity."

For the next half hour Snyder Appleby sat at his own desk, for once in his life hard at work, and feeling that he had been decidedly snubbed if not actually insulted. He was even meditating the handing in of his resignation, when the superintendent again addressed him, but this time in a much more friendly tone.

"You are from Euston, I believe?"

"Yes, sir."

"Do you happen to know a young man from there named Rodman Blake?"

"Yes, sir. I have an acquaintance there of that name," replied Snyder hesitatingly, and wondering what possible interest the "super" could have in Rod Blake. "The fact is," he added with an assumed air of frankness, "the young person in question is a sort of adopted cousin of my own; but circumstances have arisen that lead me to consider him an undesirable acquaintance."

"What are they?" inquired the superintendent bluntly.

"It would hardly be becoming in me to state them," replied Snyder, wishing he knew why the other was making these inquiries. "I should be very sorry to say anything that might injure the young man's future prospects."

"Had they anything to do with his leaving Euston, and seeking employment on this road?"

"Yes, sir; I think they had," admitted Snyder with apparent reluctance.

"Then I consider it your duty to tell me what they are," said Mr. Hill; "for I have just given young Blake the position of brakeman, and if there is any reason why he is unfit for it I should like to know it."

This aroused all the jealousy in Snyder's nature and he answered: "Well, sir, if you put it in that light, I suppose I must tell you that Blake's uncle, with whom he lived, turned him from the house without a penny in his pocket on account of his connection with a most infamous piece of rascality. But I beg that you will not question me any further on the subject. It is most painful to me to speak of even a distant connection in the terms I should be obliged to use in referring to Rodman

Blake. President Vanderveer knows the whole history of the affair, and can give you full information regarding it."

"The President has gone West on a business trip that will occupy some weeks," replied Mr. Hill, "so I could not ask him even if I were inclined to trouble him with so trifling a matter. I shall certainly investigate it, however, and if I find this young Blake to be a person of such a character as you intimate, I shall as certainly discharge him."

CHAPTER XVII.
ROD AS A BRAKEMAN.

In the meantime Rod, who was happily ignorant of this conversation, had been warmly welcomed in caboose number 18. There Conductor Tobin and the two brakemen listened with intense interest to all he had to tell them of his recent experiences. They in turn informed him of Brakeman Joe's condition, and of how the torpedoes had saved him from being run over by the night express.

He found his M. I. P. bag in the caboose where Conductor Tobin had been keeping it until he should hear from him. The conductor also handed Rod a ten dollar bill, that had been left for him by the brother of Juniper's owner, as a reward for his gallant struggle with the terrified horse in the closed car, and the subsequent care of him.

Feeling very rich and independent with this amount of money, of his own earning, at his disposal, Rod at once bought for himself a blue checkered shirt and pair of overalls, a cap, a pair of buckskin gloves with which to handle brake wheels, one of the great tin lunch-pails such as railroad men carry, and a blanket. Thus equipped he felt he was ready for any emergency. To these purchases he added a supply of provisions, and a basket of fruit that he intended to leave for Brakeman Joe when they should pass the station at which he was.

The train that they were ordered to take came along shortly before sunset. When it again pulled out, drawing caboose number 18, and with Rod Blake, brake-stick in hand, standing on the "deck" of one of its rear cars, there was no happier nor prouder lad than he in the country. How he did enjoy the novelty of that first ride on top of a freight train, and what a fine thing it seemed, to be really a railroad man. The night was clear and cold; but the exercise of setting up brakes on down grades, and throwing them off for up grades or level stretches, kept him in a glow of warmth. Then how bright and cosy the interior of the caboose, that was now his home, seemed during the occasional visits that he paid it.

Before the night grew dark, Conductor Tobin showed him how to place the two red lanterns on its rear platform, and the lights that showed red behind, green in front, and green at the side, on its upper rear corners. Then he was asked to make a fire in the little round stove, and prepare a huge pot of coffee for the train crew to drink during the night. When there was nothing else to do he might sit up in the cupola, on the side opposite to that occupied by Conductor Tobin; but on this first night he preferred taking his own lantern, and going out on "deck," as the top of the cars is called. Here he was too far from the locomotive to be annoyed by its smoke or cinders, and he loved to feel the cool night air rushing past him. He enjoyed rumbling through the depths of dark forests, and rattling over bridges or long trestles. It was strange to roll heavily through sleeping towns, where the only signs of life were the bright lights of the stations, and the twinkling red, green or white semaphore lights at the switches.

Some of the time he amused himself by holding his watch in hand, and counting the clicks of the car wheels over the rail joints; for he remembered having read that the number of rails passed in twenty seconds is almost exactly the number of miles run by a train in an hour. If it had been day time he might also have noted the number of telegraph poles passed in a minute, and calculated the speed of the train, by allowing thirty-five poles to the mile.

All this time, however, he was under orders to keep a watch on the movements of the brakemen ahead of him, and to set up, or throw off, brakes on at least two of the six cars under his charge, whenever he noticed them doing so. He was surprised to learn that it was by no means necessary to put on all the brakes of a train to check its speed, or even to stop it, and that the application of those on a third, or even a quarter of its cars answered every purpose. He also soon learned to jump quickly whenever brakes were called for by a single short whistle blast from the locomotive, and to throw them off at the order of the two short blasts that called for brakes to be loosened. At first he thought it curious that the other brakemen should run along the tops of the cars, and wondered why they were always in such a hurry. He soon discovered though that it was much easier to keep his footing running than walking, and safer to jump from car to car than to step deliberately across the open spaces between them.

Once, during the night, when he and Conductor Tobin were seated in the caboose eating their midnight lunch, the latter began to sniff the air suspiciously, and even to Rod's unaccustomed nostrils, there came a most unpleasant smell. "Hot box!" said Conductor Tobin, and the next time they stopped, they found the packing in an iron box at the end of an axle, under one of the cars, blazing at a furious rate. The journals, or bearings, in which the axle turned, had become dry and so heated by friction as to set the oil-soaked cotton waste, or packing, with which the box was filled, on fire. The job of cooling the box with buckets of water, and repacking it with waste, and thick, black, evil-smelling oil was a dirty and disagreeable one, as Rod quickly learned from experience. He also realized from what he saw, that if it were not done in time, the car itself might be set on fire, or the axle broken off.

These, and many other valuable lessons in railroading, did Rod Blake learn that night; and when in the gray dawn, the train pulled into the home yard, with its run completed, he was wiser, more sleepy and tired, than he had ever been before in all his life.

CHAPTER XVIII.
WORKING FOR A PROMOTION.

For several weeks Rod Blake continued to lead the life of a brakeman on Conductor Tobin's train. Although it was a very humble position, and though the life was one of constant danger and hard work, he thoroughly enjoyed it. Blessed with youth, health and a perfect physical condition, he even found pleasure in the stormy nights, when the running boards that formed his pathway over the roofs of the swaying cars were slippery with sleet, and fierce winds tried their best to hurl him from them. He experienced a wild joy in battling with, and conquering, gales that forced him to crawl along the storm-swept "deck" on hands and knees, clinging tightly to the running boards, often with lantern extinguished, and making the passage from car to car through pitchy darkness. On such nights how warm and cheerful was the interior of the caboose, when at rare intervals he found a chance to pay it dripping visits! How welcome were the cups of hot coffee from the steaming pot on the glowing stove, and how the appreciation of all its comforts was intensified by the wildness of the outside night!

By his unfailing cheerfulness of disposition, his promptness to answer any call, and on account of his splendid athletic training, the lad rapidly extended his circle of friendships, until there was not a trainman on the division but had a word of greeting, or a friendly wave of the hand for him, as they met at stations or were whirled past each other on the road. During the leisure "lay-off" hours at either end of the run, he gave them boxing lessons in the caboose. These proved so popular as entertainments that on such occasions the car was always crowded with eager pupils and enthusiastic spectators. In fact, before he had been a month on the road, Rod Blake had attained a popularity among the rough, but honest and manly, fellows who shared his labors, only approached by that of Smiler himself. With this wise animal he was also such a prime favorite that the dog was now more frequently to be seen on his train than on any other.

After working as rear brakeman, under Conductor Tobin's especial care, long enough to become thoroughly acquainted with his duties, Rod was, at his own request, transferred to the forward end of the train. Here he had charge of the six or eight cars immediately following the locomotive. This was not nearly so pleasant a position as that at the rear end; for now, while running, he seldom had a chance to visit the caboose, and when on duty he was directly in the path of the very worst of the smoke and cinders. Then too the work here was harder than anywhere else on the train; for, in addition to his regular duties as brakeman, he was expected to assist the fireman at water stations, and by shovelling coal down from the rear end of the tender so that it was more easily within his reach. It was for this very reason though that Rod sought the place. He did not wish to remain a brakeman very long, nor even to become a conductor; but he did want to learn how to run a locomotive, and looked forward with longing anticipation to the day when he might fill the proud position of engineman. So he shovelled coal with a hearty good-will, and seized every opportunity for riding on the locomotive, and carefully watched the movements of the men who managed it. Sometimes he asked questions, but not often; when he did they were of such a nature that the answers were of practical value to him.

From many years of riding in a locomotive cab, where, with the constant rattle and roar, conversation is very difficult, the engineman, Truman Stump, had become a most reticent man, who rarely spoke unless it was necessary. He had thus gained the reputation of being ill-tempered and morose, which was exactly what he was not. Everybody admitted, though, that he was a first-class engine-driver, and one who could always be relied upon to do exactly the thing in an emergency.

This man took a liking to the bright-faced young brakeman from the very first; and, when Rod began to appear in his cab, he watched him with a real, but concealed interest. One day when it was announced that Milt Sturgis, the fireman, was about to be promoted and get his engine, everybody wondered who would take his place, and how a new man would get along with old True Stump. Another bit of news received on the train at the the same time, was that Brakeman Joe had fully recovered from his injuries, and was ready to resume his place. While Rod was glad, for Joe's sake, that he was well enough to come back, he could not help feeling some anxiety on his own account, now that he would no longer be needed as brakeman. This anxiety was unexpectedly relieved by the engineman; who, while standing beside him at a water station, turned and said:

"Joe's coming back."

"Yes; to-morrow."

"Milt's going to leave."

"So I hear."

"How would you like to fire for me in his place?"

"I," exclaimed Rod in astonishment. "Why, I should like it very much if you think I know enough for the job."

"All right, I'll fix it."

CHAPTER XIX.
THE EXPRESS SPECIAL.

Nothing further was said at the time concerning Rod's most cherished scheme and as Brakeman Joe reported for duty that very day Rod was at a loss to know what he should do next. He doubted if Truman Stump could command sufficient influence to secure his appointment as fireman before he had undergone a preliminary training as wiper and hostler in the round-house, though he felt that he already possessed experience as valuable as any to be gained in those positions. Still it was a rule that firemen should be taken from the round-house and Rod knew by this time that railroad rules are rarely broken.

Of course he could not retain Joe's position now that the latter had returned to it, and he would not if he could. No indeed! Joe's face still pale from his long confinement was too radiant with happiness at once more getting back among his old friends and associations for Rod to dim it by the faintest suggestion that the honest fellow's return to duty was likely to throw him out of a job. So he congratulated Joe upon his recovery, as heartily as any one, and retold the story of his plucky fight with the thieving tramps to the little group of railroad men gathered in caboose number 18 to welcome him back.

As they were all talking at once and making a hero of Brakeman Joe they were hushed into a sudden silence by the unexpected entrance of Mr. Hill the Superintendent. Merely nodding to the others this gentleman stepped up to Brakeman Joe with extended hand, saying cordially:

"Good evening, conductor. I am glad to see you back among us again. I hope you are all right and will be able to take your train out on time to-night."

"Sir! I----" stammered the astonished Joe.

"You must be mistaking me for Conductor Tobin, sir."

"Tobin? oh no! I know him too well ever to mistake any one else for him. I take you to be Conductor Joseph Miller of the through freight, whose promotion has just been posted, to take effect immediately. I have also assigned two new men to your train, with orders to report at once. Here they come now."

This announcement fell like a bomb-shell; and the cheer of congratulation that Joe's friends attempted to raise was checked, half-uttered, by the distressed look on Conductor Tobin's face. Could it be that he had heard aright? Was it possible that he was thus unceremoniously thrown out of work to make a place for his former brakeman? His expression was quite as bewildered as that of Brakeman Joe, and the Superintendent, noticing it, allowed an amused smile to flit across his own face.

"Don't be alarmed, Tobin," he said, reassuringly; "the Company can't very well spare your services, and have no idea of doing so. If you can make it convenient I should like to have you take out number 29 to-night, and, as you will need an extra hand, I have decided to send young Blake on the same train; that is, if it will be agreeable to you to have him."

Number 29! The Continental Express Company's Special! Why, only passenger conductors had that train! What could Mr. Hill mean?

"It's all right, Tobin," continued that gentleman, noting the other's embarrassment; "your name has gone on to the passenger list, and if you do as well there as you have with your freights I shall be more than satisfied. I hope this change strikes you as being one for the better also?" he added, turning to Rod.

"Yes, sir, only----" began Rodman, who was about to say something concerning his desire to be made a fireman, when he suddenly remembered that Truman Stump had requested him not to speak of it just yet.

"Only what?" asked Mr. Hill, a little sharply.

"I was afraid I hadn't experience enough," answered Rod.

"That is a matter of which I claim to be the best judge," replied the Superintendent, with a smile. "And if I am satisfied of your fitness for the position you certainly ought to be. Now, Tobin, look lively. Number 29 must be ready to leave in half an hour. Good-night and good luck to you."

Thus Conductor Tobin's long and faithful service, and Brakeman Joe's suffering, and Rod Blake's strict attention to duty were all rewarded at once, though in Rodman's case the reward had not taken exactly the shape he desired. Still, a promotion was a promotion, and where there were so many competitors for each upward step, as there always are on a railroad, it was not for him to grumble at the form in which it came.

So as the young railroad man gathered up his few belongings, he gratefully accepted the congratulations of his friends. A few minutes later he bade freight conductor Joe good-by, and in company with passenger conductor Tobin he left caboose number 18 with much the same feeling that a young scholar leaves his primary school for one a grade higher.

Number 29 was a peculiar train, and one that Rod had often watched rush past his side-tracked freight with feelings of deep interest, not unmixed with envy. It always followed the "Limited," with all the latter's privileges of precedence and right of way. Thus it was such a flyer that the contrast between it and the freight, which always had to get out of the way, was as great as that between a thorough-bred racer and a farm-horse. It was made up of express cars, loaded with money, jewelry, plate, and other valuable packages, which caused it to be known along the road as the "gold mine." In its money-car was carried specie and bank notes from the United States Treasury, and from Eastern banks to Western cities. Thus it was no unusual thing for this one car to carry a million dollars' worth of such express matter. Each car was in charge of a trusted and well-armed messenger, who locked himself in from one end of his run to the other, and was prepared to defend the valuables entrusted to his care with his life. Thus number 29 was one of the most important as well as one of the very fastest trains on the road; while to run on it was considered such an honor that many envious glances were cast at Rod as he stood on the platform beside it awaiting the starting-signal.

There had been no time for him to procure the blue uniform suit, such as the crews of passenger trains, with whom he now ranked, are required to wear; and as the jumper and overalls of a freight brakeman would have been decidedly out of place on an express special, Rod had hastily donned his best suit of every-day clothes. Thus as he stood near the steps of the single passenger coach that was attached to the train in place of a caboose for the accommodation of its conductor and brakemen, he was not to be distinguished from the throng of passengers hastening aboard the "Limited" on the opposite side of the platform.

For this reason a young man, with a stout leather travelling bag slung on his shoulder, paid no attention to the young brakeman, as after a hurried glance up and down the platform, he sprang aboard and entered the coach.

With a bound Rod was after him. "Hello, sir!" he cried; "you must have made a mistake. This is not a passenger train."

"No?" said the other coolly, and Rod now noticed that he wore a pair of smoked glasses. I thought it was the "Limited."

"That is the 'Limited,' across the platform," explained Rod politely.

"Are you sure of it?"

"Certainly I am."

"What makes you think this is not it?" asked the other with a provoking slowness of speech as though time was no object to him, and he did not care whether the "Limited" started without him or not.

"Because I belong on this train and it is my business to be sure of things connected with it," replied Rod, still speaking pleasantly.

"Oh, you do, do you. Are you its conductor?"

"No, sir, but I am one of its brakemen."

"Are there any more like you?"

"Yes, sir, there is another like me. I sha'n't need his help though to put you off this train if you don't get off, and in a hurry too," answered Rod hotly, for he began to suspect that the young man was making fun of him.

"Oh, come now!" said the passenger mildly, "don't get excited, I'm perfectly willing to go. It was a very natural mistake for a blind man to make. You may be blind yourself some day, and then you'll find out."

"I didn't know you were blind, sir," exclaimed Rod apologetically and instantly regretting his harshness toward one so cruelly afflicted. "I am very sorry, and if you will allow me, I will see you safely aboard the 'Limited.'"

The young man accepted this offer, explaining at the same time that while he was not totally blind, his sight was very dim. So Rod helped him off one train and into the other, striving by every attention to atone for the abruptness with which he had spoken before learning of the other's infirmity. As he took the stranger's hand to guide him down the steps of the coach he noticed that the large diamond of a ring worn by the latter, had cut its way through the back of one of his kid gloves.

A moment later the "Limited" pulled out, and in a few minutes the express special, laden that night with a freight of unusual value, followed it.

CHAPTER XX.
TROUBLE IN THE MONEY CAR.

Until after midnight the run of the express special was without interruption or incident. Thus far it had made but two stops. The second of these was at the end of the freight division where Conductor Tobin had been accustomed to turn over his train to a relieving crew and spend the day. With such a flyer as the special, however, his run was now to be twice as long as formerly, so that he and Rod looked forward to doing a hundred and fifty miles more before being relieved. There was but one other brakeman besides Rod, and as there was little for either of them to do, save to see that the rear end lights burned brightly, and always to be prepared for emergencies, time hung rather heavily on their hands.

Thanks to automatic air brakes, the life of a passenger brakeman is now a very easy one as compared with the same life a few years ago. The brakeman of those days, almost as greasy and smoke begrimed as a fireman, spent most of his time on the swaying platforms between cars amid showers of cinders and clouds of blinding dust. At every call for brakes he was obliged to spring to the wheels of the two entrusted to his care and set them up by hand with the utmost exercise of his strength. He was not allowed to remain inside the cars between stations, and the only glimpses he got of their scant comfort was when he flung open their doors to call out the names of stations in his own undistinguishable jargon. He was invariably a well-grown powerfully built fellow, as rough in manner as in appearance.

To-day, on all passenger trains and on many freights as well, the automatic brakes are operated by compressed air controlled by the engineman. By a single pull of a small brass lever within easy reach he can instantly apply every brake on his train with such force as to bring it to a standstill inside of a few seconds. The two small cylinders connected by a piston-rod on the right hand side of every locomotive just in front of the cab form the air-pump. It is always at work while a train is standing still, forcing air through lengths of rubber hose between the cars and into the reservoirs located beneath each one. As brakes are applied by the reduction of this air the engineman's lever merely opens a valve that allows the imprisoned force to escape with a sharp hissing sound. If a train should break in two the connecting lengths of rubber hose would be torn asunder, and the outrushing air would instantly apply brakes to the cars of both sections bringing them to a speedy standstill.

Thus the brakeman of to-day, instead of being the powerful, cinder-coated and rough-voiced fellow of a few years back, may be as slim and elegant as any of the passengers under his care provided he is polite, wide-awake, and attentive to his duty. Clad in a natty uniform, he now spends his time inside the car instead of on its platform. He has reports to make out, lamps and flags to look after, and in cases of unexpected delay must run back to protect his train from any other that may be approaching it. Formerly it was necessary to have as many brakemen on a passenger train as there were cars, while now it is rare to find more than two on each train.

So Rod had very little to do in his new position, and soon after leaving the second stopping-place of his train, was sitting near the forward end of the coach with his head resting on the back of a seat, gazing at the ceiling and buried in deep thought. Conductor Tobin and the other brakeman were seated some distance behind him engaged in conversation.

Rod was thinking of what an awful thing it was to be blind, and this chain of thought was suggested by a glimpse of the young man with smoked glasses, whom he had assisted on board the "Limited" some hours before, standing on the platform of the station they had just left. He had evidently reached his journey's end and was patiently waiting for some one to come and lead him away--or at least this was what Rod imagined the situation to be. In reality, that same young man, with unimpaired eyesight and no longer wearing smoked glasses, was on board the express special at that very moment. He had sprung on to the forward platform of the money car undetected in the darkness as the train left the circle of station lights and was now on its roof fastening a light rope ladder to a ledge just above one of the middle and half-glazed doors of the car. A red flannel mask concealed the lower half of his face, and as he swung himself down on his frail and fearfully swaying support he held a powerful navy revolver in his right hand. He was taking frightful risks to win a desperate game. Failing in his effort to conceal himself aboard the very train he intended to rob, he had taken passage on the "Limited" as far as its first stopping-place and had there awaited the coming of the Express Special. Thus far his reckless venture had succeeded, and as Rod sat in the coach thinking pityingly of him, he was covering the unsuspecting messenger in the money car with his revolver.

"What would I do if I were blind?" thought Rod. "I suppose uncle would take care of me; but how humiliating it would be to have to go back to him helpless and dependent. How thankful I should be that I can see besides being well and strong and able to care for myself. I will do it too without asking help from any one, and I'll win such a name for honesty and faithfulness on this road that even Uncle Arms will be compelled to believe whatever I may tell him. I wonder if Snyder could have put that emery into the oil-cup himself? It doesn't seem as though any one could be so mean."

Just here a slight incident interrupted the lad's thoughts so suddenly that he sprang to his feet--unconsciously his eyes had been fixed on the bell-cord that ran through the entire train to the cab of the locomotive. It had hung a little slack, but all at once this slack was jerked up as though some one had pulled the cord. This would have been a signal to stop the train, and if the train were to be stopped at that point something must be wrong. A backward glance showed Conductor Tobin and the other brakeman to be still quietly engaged in conversation. Neither of them could have pulled the cord. Rod stepped to the door and looked out. The train was tearing along at a terrific speed, and the rush of air nearly took away his breath. There was no sign of slackening speed and everything appeared to be all right. The next car ahead of the coach was the money car. At least Conductor Tobin had thought so, though none of the trainmen was ever quite sure which one of the half dozen or more express cars it was. Its rear door was of course closed and locked, but some impulse moved Rod to clamber up on its platform railing and peer through the little hole by which the bell-cord entered. He could not see much, but that which was disclosed in a single glimpse almost caused his heart to cease its beating. Within his range of vision came the heads of two men evidently engaged in a struggle and one of them wore a mask over the lower part of his face. The next instant Rod had sprung down from his perilous perch and dashed back into the coach shouting breathlessly:

"There's a masked man fighting the messenger in the money car!"

CHAPTER XXI.
OVER THE TOP OF THE TRAIN.

At Rodman's startling announcement Conductor Tobin sprang to his feet, reached for the bell-cord, and gave it two sharp pulls. A single whistle blast from the locomotive made instant reply that his signal was received and understood. So promptly was it obeyed that as the conductor and his two brakemen ran to the front platform to swing far out and look along the sides of the express cars ahead of them, the grinding brakes were already reducing the speed of the flying train.

Suddenly a pistol shot rang angrily out, and a bullet crashed into the woodwork close above Rod Blake's head. He and the conductor were leaning out on one side while the other brakeman occupied the opposite one.

"Give the signal to go ahead at once, or I'll come back there and blow your brains out!" came in a hoarse voice from a side door of the money car.

"All right, I'll do it; only don't shoot," shouted Conductor Tobin in answer, giving the desired signal to the engineman, by raising and lowering his lantern vertically, as he spoke. At the same time he said hurriedly to the brakeman on the opposite side of the platform, and thus concealed from the robber's view:

"Drop off, Tom, and run back to number 10. Telegraph ahead to all stations, and we'll bag that fellow yet!"

The man did as directed, swinging low and giving a forward spring that landed him safely beside the track, though the train was still moving fully twenty miles an hour.

The engineman, though greatly puzzled at receiving the signal to go ahead immediately after being ordered to stop, had obeyed it, thrown off brakes, and the train was again gathering its usual headway.

"Now Rod," said Conductor Tobin, as the other brakeman disappeared; "I want you to make your way over the top of the train to the engine, and tell Eli what is taking place. Tell him to keep her wide open till we reach Millbank, and not to give her the "air" till we are well up with the station. It's a tough job for you, and one I hate to send you on. At the same time it's got to be done, and after your experience on the freight deck, I believe you are the lad to undertake it. Anyway, you'll be safe from that pistol when once you reach the cab."

"But I don't like to leave you here alone to be shot," remonstrated Rod.

"Never mind me. I don't believe I'll get shot. At any rate, this is my place, and here I must stay. Now move along, and God bless you."

There was a strong hand-clasp between the conductor and brakeman, and then the latter started on the perilous journey he had been ordered to undertake. It was no easy task to maintain a footing on the rounded roofs of those express cars as they were hurled on through the night at the rate of nearly a mile a minute; while to leap from one to another seemed almost suicidal. Not more than one brakeman in a thousand could have done it; but Rod Blake, with his light weight, athletic training, and recent experience combined with absolute fearlessness, was that one. His inclination was to get down on his hands and knees and crawl along the slippery roofs. If he had yielded to it he would never have accomplished the trip. He believed that the only way to make it was by running and clearing the spaces between cars with flying leaps, and, incredible as it may seem, that is the way he did it. He had kicked off his shoes before starting, and now ran with stockinged feet.

The occupants of the cab were as startled by his appearance beside them as though he had been a ghost, and when his story was told the engineman wanted to stop the train at once and go back to the assistance of the imperilled messenger. Rod however succeeded in persuading him that, as the messenger's fate was probably already decided, their only hope of capturing the robber lay in carrying out Conductor Tobin's plan of running at such speed that he would not dare jump from the train until a station prepared for his reception was reached.

When the engineman finally agreed to this, and before he could utter the remonstrance that sprang to his lips, Rodman clambered back over the heaped-up coal of the tender, swung himself to the roof of the forward car and began to retrace his perilous journey to the rear end of the train. He argued that if Conductor Tobin's place was back there exposed to the shots of a desperate man, his brakeman's place was beside him. Even if Rod had not been a railroad boy, or "man," as he now called himself, his natural bravery and sense of honor would have taken him back to that coach. Ever since he had enlisted in the service that demands as strict obedience as that required of a soldier and an equal contempt of danger, this lad was doubly alert to the call of whatever he regarded as duty. There is no service in the world, outside of the army, so nearly resembling it in requirements and discipline as that of a railroad. It is no place for cowards nor weaklings; but to such a lad as Rod Blake it adds the stimulus of excitement and ever-present danger and the promise of certain promotion and ample reward for the conscientious performance of every-day duties.

So Rod, feeling in duty bound to do so, made his way back over the reeling roofs of that on-rushing train to the side of his superior officer. As he scrambled and slipped and leaped from car to car he fully realized the imminent peril of his situation, but was at the same time filled with a wild exhilaration and buoyance of spirits such as he had never before known.

Conductor Tobin, standing just inside the coach door with pale face and set lips, was amazed to see him. For a moment he fancied the lad had been daunted by the task imposed upon him and had turned back without reaching the locomotive. When he realized that Rod had not only made the perilous trip once, but twice, his admiration was unbounded, and though he tried to scold him for his foolhardiness the words refused to come. He shook the young brakeman's hand so heartily instead that the action conveyed a volume of praise and appreciation.

Now, as they watched together with an intense eagerness for the lights of Millbank they became conscious of a yellow glare, like that of an open furnace, streaming from the side door of the money car.

"The scoundrel has set the car on fire!" gasped Conductor Tobin.

"Don't you think we ought to break in the door with an axe and make a rush for him?" asked Rod.

Before the other could reply, a long, ear-splitting whistle blast announcing their approach to a station sounded from the locomotive.

CHAPTER XXII.
STOP THIEF!

As Train Number 29 dashed up to the Millbank station and was brought to a stop almost as suddenly as a spirited horse is reined back on his haunches by a curb bit, the many flashing lanterns guarding all approaches, and the confused throng of dark forms on its platform told that Brakeman Tom had performed his duty and that its arrival was anticipated.

The abruptness of this unexpected stop caused the messengers in the several cars to open their doors and look out inquiringly. At the same time, and even before it was safe to do so, Conductor Tobin and Rod dropped to the ground and ran to the door of the money car. The glare of firelight streaming from it attracted others to the same spot. There were loud cries for buckets and water, and almost before the car wheels ceased to slide on the polished rails a score of willing hands were drenching out the fire of way-bills, other papers, and a broken chair that was blazing merrily in the middle of its floor. The flames were already licking the interior woodwork, and but for this opportune stop would have gathered such headway inside of another minute as would not only have destroyed the car but probably the entire train.

The moment the subsiding flames rendered such a thing possible, a rush was made for the inside of the car, but Conductor Tobin calling one of the express messengers and the engineman who had come running back, to aid him, and telling Rod to guard the door, sternly ordered the crowd to keep out until he had made an examination. From his post at the doorway Rod could look in at a sight that filled him with horror. The interior of the car was spattered with blood. On the floor, half hidden beneath a pile of packages, lay the messenger, still alive but unconscious and bleeding from half a dozen wounds. The brave right hand that had tried to pull the bell cord had been shattered by a pistol ball, and the messenger's own Winchester lay on the floor beside him. Broken packages that had contained money, jewelry, and other valuables were scattered in every direction, while the open safe from which they had come was as empty as the day it was made.

The trainmen became furious as one after another of these mute witnesses told of the outrages so recently perpetrated, and swore vengeance on the robber when they should catch him. They ransacked every corner of the car, but search as they might they could discover no trace of his presence nor of the method of his flight. The man had left the car as he had entered it taking the precaution of removing his rope ladder as he went.

The baffled searchers had just reached the conclusion that he must have leaped from the train in spite of its speed and of Conductor Tobin's watchfulness, when Rod, who from his position in the doorway could look over the heads of the crowd surrounding the car called out:

"Stop that man! The one with a leather bag slung over his shoulder! Stop him! Stop thief! He is the robber!"

In the glare of an electric light that happened to shine full upon him for a moment, Rod had seen the man walk away from the forward end of the car next ahead of the one they were searching as though he had just left it. He was not noticed by the bystanders as all eyes were directed toward the door of the money car. To the young brakeman his figure and the stout leather bag that he carried seemed familiar. As he looked, the man raised a kid-gloved hand to shift the position of his satchel, and from it shot the momentary flash of a diamond. With Rod this was enough to at once establish the man's identity. Although he no longer wore smoked glasses Rod knew him to be the man who, pretending partial blindness, had first boarded the Express Special, then taken passage on the "Limited," and whom he had seen on the platform of the last station at which they had stopped. How could he have reached Millbank? He must have come by the Express Special, and so must be connected with its robbery.

All these thoughts darted through Rod's head like a flash of lightning, and as he uttered his shouts of warning he sprang to the ground with a vague idea of preventing the stranger's escape. At the same moment the crowd surged back upon him, and when he finally cleared himself from it he saw the man backing down the platform, holding his would-be pursuers in check with a levelled pistol, and just disappearing from the circle of electric light.

A minute later two frightened men were driven at the point of a revolver from the cab of a freight locomotive that, under a full head of steam, was standing on the outer one of the two west-bound tracks. They had hardly left it in sole charge of the robber, by whom it had already been uncoupled from its train, before it sprang forward and began to move away through the darkness.

Rod, who was now well in advance of all other pursuers, instantly comprehended the situation. His own train stood on the inner west-bound track and he was near its forward end. The robber with his blood-stained plunder was disappearing before his very eyes, and if lost to view might easily run on for a few miles and then make good his escape. He must not be allowed to do so! He must be kept in sight!

This was Rod's all-absorbing thought at the moment. Moved by it, he jerked out the coupling-pin, by which the locomotive of the Express Special was attached to its train, leaped into the cab, threw over the lever, pulled open the throttle, and had started on one of the most thrilling races recorded in the annals of railroading, before the astonished fireman, who had been left in charge, found time to remonstrate.

"Look here, young fellow! what are you about?" he shouted, stepping threateningly toward Rod.

"We are about chasing the train robber, who has just gone off with that engine on number four track, and you want to keep up the best head of steam you know how," was the answer.

"Have we any orders to do so?"

"You have, at any rate, for I give them to you."

"And who are you? I never saw you before to-night."

"I am Rod Blake, one of Tobin's trainmen, and if you don't quit bothering me with your stupidity and go to work, I'll pitch you out of this cab!" shouted Rod savagely, in a tone that betrayed the intensity of his nervous excitement.

The man had heard of the young brakeman and of his skill as a boxer, though he had never met him before that night, and his half-formed intention of compelling the lad to turn back was decidedly weakened by the mention of his name. Still he hesitated. He was a powerful fellow with whom in a struggle Rod could not have held his own for a minute, but he was clearly lacking in what railroad men call "sand." Suddenly Rod made a movement as though to spring at him, at the same time shouting, "Do as I tell you, sir, and get to work at once!"

CHAPTER XXIII.
A RACE OF LOCOMOTIVES.

In any struggle between two human beings, the one possessed of the more powerful will is certain to win. In the present case, Rod Blake's will was so much stronger than that of the fireman that the burly fellow obeyed his order, turned sullenly away, and began to shovel coal into the roaring furnace.

Their speed was now tremendous, for though Rod knew but little about the management of a locomotive engine, he did know that the wider the throttle was opened the faster it would go. So he pulled the handle as far back as he dared, and soon had the satisfaction of seeing the dark form of the fugitive locomotive disclosed by the glare of their own head-light. Now if he could keep it in sight, and so force the speed, that it would be impossible for the robber to jump off until some large station was reached, Rod felt that all would yet go well.

Suddenly the runaway seemed to stop. Then it began to move back toward them. In another instant they had dashed past it, but not before two pistol bullets had come crashing through the cab windows. A bit of splintered glass cut Rod's forehead and a little stream of blood began to trickle down his face. Without heeding it, he shut off steam, reversed, opened again, and within half a minute the pursuers were rushing back over the ground they had just covered.

Again the train robber tried the same game, again the two locomotives flew by each other, and again pistol balls came singing past Rod Blake's ears. As for the fireman he had flung himself flat on the floor of the cab. Rod could hardly believe that he had not been hit by one of those hissing bullets, but as he felt no wound he again reversed his engine and again dashed ahead.

Now they gained steadily on the fugitive. His steam was giving out, and he had neither the time to renew his supply nor the knowledge of how to do so. The pursuit was decidedly hotter than he had anticipated, and had not been checked in the least by his pistol shots, as he had hoped it would be. He must try some other plan of escape, and that quickly. He did not know how many men were on that fiercely pursuing locomotive, nor whether they were armed or not. He only knew that within another minute they would overtake him. He formed a desperate resolve, and a moment later Rod Blake thought he saw a dark form scrambling from a ditch beside the track as they flew past. When they reached the "dying" locomotive of which they were in pursuit and found it abandoned, he knew what had taken place. The train robber had leaped from its cab and was now making his way across country on foot.

"We must follow him!" exclaimed Rod.

"You may if you are such a fool; but I'll be blowed if I will," answered the fireman.

There was no time to be lost in argument, neither was Rod sure that those locomotives ought to be left unguarded. So, without another word, he dropped to the ground and started on a run across the fields in the direction he was almost certain the fugitive had taken.

The young brakeman soon came to a wagon road running parallel to the railway. Here he was brought to a halt. Which way should he go? To attempt to continue the pursuit in either direction without some definite knowledge to act upon seemed foolish. If he could only discover a house at which to make inquiries, or if some belated traveller would only come that way.

"'Belated traveller' is good," mused Rod as his eye caught a faint glow in the eastern sky. "Here it is almost to-morrow while I thought it was still to-day. What a wild-goose chase I have come on anyway, and what should I do if I overtook the robber? I'm sure I don't know. I won't give it up though now that I have started in on it. Hello! Here comes some one now. Perhaps I can learn something from him. Hi, there!"

The sound that had attracted the lad's attention was that of a rapidly galloping horse, though it was so deadened by the sandy road that he did not hear it until the animal was close upon him. The light was very dim, and as Rod stood in a shadow neither the horse nor its rider perceived him until he started forward and shouted to attract the latter's attention.

In an instant the startled animal had sprung to one side so suddenly as to fling its rider violently to the ground, where he lay motionless. The horse ran a short distance, then stopped and stood trembling.

Horrified at the result of his hasty action, Rod kneeled beside the motionless man. His head had struck the root of a tree and though the boy could not discover that he was seriously injured, he was unconscious. In vain did the distressed lad attempt to restore him. He had little idea of what to do, there was no water at hand, and to his ignorance it seemed as if the man must be dying. He lifted one of the limp hands to chafe it, and started with amazement at the sight of a diamond ring that had cut its way through the torn and blackened kid glove in which the hand was encased.

Could this be the very train robber of whom he was in pursuit? Where, then, was his leather satchel? Why, there it was, only a few feet away, lying where it had fallen as the man was flung to the ground. Incredible as it seemed, this must be the very man, and now what was to be done? Was ever a fellow placed in a more perplexing situation? He could not revive the unconscious form. Neither could he remove it from that place. Clearly he must have help. As he arrived at this conclusion Rod started on a run down the road, determined to find a habitation and secure human aid.

CHAPTER XXIV.
ARRESTED ON SUSPICION.

As Rod started on his quest for assistance the riderless horse, which had begun to nibble grass by the roadside, lifted his head with a snort that brought the lad to a sudden halt. Why not make use of this animal if he could catch it? Certainly his mission could be accomplished more quickly on horseback than on foot. He started gently toward it, holding out his hand and speaking soothingly; but the cautious animal tossed its head and began to move away. "How much he resembles Juniper," thought Rod. "Here, Juniper! Here June, old fellow!" he called. At the sound of his name the horse wheeled about and faced the lad in whose company he had recently undergone such a thrilling experience. The next instant Rod grasped the animal's halter, for it had neither saddle nor bridle, and Juniper was evidently recognizing him.

As the young brakeman was about to leap on the horse's back it occurred to him that the leather bag, which was undoubtedly filled with valuable plunder from the rifled express car ought not to be left lying in the road. No, it would be much better to carry it to a place of safety. With this thought came a recollection of the pistol shots so lately fired by the man at his feet. Would it not be well to disarm him lest he should revive and again prove dangerous before assistance could be found and brought to the place. Rod believed it would, and, acting upon the thought, transferred two revolvers from the train-robber's pockets to his own. Then, after dragging the still unconscious man a little to one side beyond danger from any wagon that might happen along, the lad slung the heavy satchel over his shoulder, scrambled on to Juniper's back and galloped away.

The road was a lonely one, and he rode more than a mile before reaching a farm-house. Here the excited lad rapped loudly on the front door and shouted. No one was yet astir, and several minutes passed before an upper window was cautiously opened and a woman's voice inquired who was there and what was wanted.

Rod began to explain his errand; but after a few words the woman called to him to wait until she could come down, and then slammed the window down. To the young brakeman's impatience the ensuing delay seemed an hour in length, though in reality not more than five minutes elapsed before the front door opened and the woman again appeared.

"Now, what were you trying to tell me about men dying in the road?" she asked sharply.

As Rod was about to reply there came a sound of galloping horses and a shout from the place where he had left Juniper fastened to a fence post.

"There he is!"

"Now we've got him!"

"Throw up your hands, you scoundrel!"

"Don't you dare draw a pistol or we'll fill you full of holes!"

These and a score of similar cries came to the ears of the bewildered lad as half a dozen horsemen dashed up to the front gate, and four of them, leaping to the ground, ran towards him while the others held the horses.

He was too astonished even to remonstrate, and as they seized him he submitted to the indignity as quietly as one who is dazed.

The woman in the doorway regarded this startling scene with amazement. When in answer to her eager questions the new-comers told her that the young desperado whom she had so nearly admitted to her house was a horse-thief, who, but a short time before, had stolen the animal now tied to her front fence, at the point of a revolver from the man who was leading him to water, she said she wouldn't have believed that such a mere boy could be so great a villian.

"It's the truth though," affirmed the man who acted as spokesman. "Isn't it, Al?"

"Yes, siree," replied Al, a heavy-looking young farm hand. "An more 'n that, he fired at me too afore I'd give up the 'orse. Oh, yes, he's a bad un, young as he looks, an hangin' wouldn't be none too good for him."

"I did nothing of the kind!" cried Rod, indignantly, now finding a chance to speak. "This is an outrage, and----"

"Is this the fellow, Al?" asked the spokesman, interrupting the young brakeman's vehement protest.

"Of course it is. I'd know him anywhere by that bag slung over his shoulders, an he's got pistols in his pockets, too."

"Yes, here they are," replied the leader, thrusting his hands into Rod's coat pockets and drawing forth the two revolvers. "Oh, there's no use talking, young man. The proof against you is too strong. The only thing for you to do is to come along quietly and make the best of the situation. Horse thieves have been getting altogether too plenty in this part of the country of late, and we've been laying for one to make an example of for more 'n a week now. Its mighty lucky for you that you didn't tackle an armed man instead of Al there, this morning. If you had you'd have got a bullet instead of a horse."

"But I tell you," cried Rod, "that I took those things from a man who was flung from that horse back here in the road about a mile. He is----"

"I haven't any doubt that you took them," interrupted the man, grimly, "the same as you took the horse."

"And I only made use of the horse to obtain assistance for him the more quickly," continued Rod. "I left him stunned by his fall, and he may be dead by this time. He will be soon, anyway, if some one doesn't go to him, and then you'll be murderers, that's what you'll be."

"Let us examine this bag that you admit you took from somebody without his permission, and see what it contains," said the man quietly, paying no heed to the lad's statement. So saying, he opened the satchel that still hung from Rod's shoulders. At the sight of its contents he uttered an exclamation of amazement.

"Well, if this don't beat anything I ever heard of!"

The others crowded eagerly about him.

"Whew! look at the greenbacks!" cried one.

"And gold!" shouted another.

"He must have robbed a bank!"

"There'll be a big reward offered for this chap."

"He's a more desperate character than we thought."

"A regular jail-bird!"

"There's blood on some of these bills!"

"He ought to be tied."

This last sentiment met with such general approval that some one produced a bit of rope, and in another moment poor Rod's hands were securely bound together behind him.

CHAPTER XXV.
THE TRAIN ROBBER LEARNS OF ROD'S ARREST.

"I tell you the man who did it all is lying back there in the road!" screamed Rod, furious with indignation at this outrage and almost sobbing with the bitterness of his distress. "He is a train robber, and I'm a passenger brakeman on the New York and Western road. He made an escape and I was chasing him."

"Just listen to that now," said one of the men jeeringly. "It's more than likely you are the train robber yourself."

"Looks like a brakeman, doesn't he?" sneered another, "especially as they are all obliged to wear a uniform when on duty."

"He's a nice big party of men, he is. Just such a one as the railroad folks would collect and send in pursuit of a train robber," remarked the leader ironically. "Oh, no, my lad, that's too thin. If you must tell lies I'd advise you to invent some that folks might have a living chance of believing."

"It's not a lie!" declared Rod earnestly and almost calmly; for though his face was quite pale with suppressed excitement, he was regaining control of his voice. "It's the solemn truth and I'm willing to swear to it."

"Oh, hush, sonny, don't swear. That would be naughty," remonstrated one of the men, mockingly.

Without noticing him, Rod continued: "If you will only take me back about a mile on the road I will show you the real train robber, and so prove that part of my story. Then at Millbank I can prove the rest."

"Look here, young fellow," said the leader, harshly, "why will you persist in such nonsense? We have just came over that part of the road and we didn't see anything of any man lying in it."

"Because I dragged him to one side," explained Rod.

"Oh, well, you'll have a chance to show us your man if you can find him, for we are going to take you back that way anyhow. Come on, fellows, let's be moving. The sooner we get this young horse-thief behind bolts and bars the sooner we'll be rid of an awkward responsibility."

So poor Rod, still bound, was placed on Juniper's back, and, with one man on each side of him, two in front and two behind, rode unhappily back over the road that he had traversed on an errand of mercy but a short time before.

As the little group disappeared, the woman in whose front yard this exciting arrest had been made turned to hasten the preparations for her children's breakfast that she might the sooner visit her nearest neighbors and tell them of these wonderful happenings. She was filled with the belief that she had had a most remarkable escape, and was eager to have her theory confirmed.

When she finally reached her neighbor's house and burst in upon them breathless and unannounced, she was somewhat taken aback to see a strange young man, wearing a pair of smoked glasses and having a very pale face, sitting at breakfast with them. The woman of the house informed her in a whisper, that he was a poor theological student making his way on foot back to college in order to save travelling expenses, and though he had only stopped to ask for a glass of water they had insisted upon his taking breakfast with them.

Then the visitor unburdened herself of her budget of startling news, ending up with: "An' I knew he was a desp'rate character the minit I set eyes onto him, for I'm a master-hand at reading faces, I am. Why, sir," here she turned to the pale student by whose evident interest in her story she was greatly flattered, "I could no more take him for the honest lad he claimed to be than I would take you for a train robber. No, indeed. A face is like a printed page to me every time and I'm not likely to be fooled, I can tell you."

"It is truly a wonderful gift," murmured the young man as he rose from the table and started to leave the house, excusing his haste on the plea of having a long distance still to travel.

"What a saintly expression that young man has!" exclaimed the visitor, watching him out of sight, "and what a preacher he will make!"

At the same moment he of the smoked glasses was saying to himself: "So that is what happened while I lay there like a log by the roadside, is it? Well, it's hard luck; but certainly I ought to be able to turn the information furnished by that silly woman to some good account."

In the meantime poor Rod was far from enjoying a morning ride that under other circumstances would have proved delightful. The sun shone from an unclouded sky, the air was deliciously cool and bracing, and the crisp autumn leaves of the forest-road rustled pleasantly beneath the horses' feet. But the boy was thinking too intently, and his thoughts were of too unpleasant a nature for him to take note of these things. He was wondering what would happen in case the train robber should not be found where he had left him.

He was not left long in suspense, for when they reached the place that he was certain was the right one there was no man, unconscious or otherwise, to be seen on either side or in any direction. He had simply regained his senses soon after Rod left him, staggered to his feet, and, with ever increasing strength, walked slowly along the road. He finally discovered a side path through the woods that led him to the farm-house where, on account of his readily concocted tale, he received and accepted a cordial invitation to breakfast.

As for Rod, his disappointment at not finding the proof of which he had been so confident was so great that he hardly uttered a protest, when instead of carrying him to Millbank or any other station on the line where he might have found friends, his captors turned into a cross-road from the left and journeyed directly away from the railroad.

In about an hour they reached the village of Center where the young brakeman, escorted by half the population of the place, was conducted through the main street to the county jail. Here he was delivered to the custody of the sheriff with such an account of his terrible deeds, and strict injunctions as to his safe keeping, that the official locked him into the very strongest of all his cells. As the heavy door clanged in his face, and Rod realized that he was actually a prisoner, he vaguely wondered if railroad men often got into such scrapes while attempting the faithful discharge of their duties.

CHAPTER XXVI.
A WELCOME VISITOR.

To be cast into jail and locked up in a cell is not a pleasant experience even for one who deserves such a fate; while to an honest lad like Rodman Blake who had only tried to perform what he considered his duty to the best of his ability, it was terrible. In vain did he assure himself that his friends would soon discover his predicament and release him from it. He could not shake off the depressing influence of that narrow room, of the forbidding white walls, and the grim grating of the massive door. He was too sensible to feel any sense of disgrace in being thus wrongfully imprisoned; but the horror of the situation remained, and it seemed as though he should suffocate behind those bars if not speedily released.

In the meantime the sheriff, whose breakfast had been interrupted by the arrival of the self-appointed constables and their prisoner, returned to his own pleasant dining-room to finish that meal. He was a bachelor, and the only other occupant of the room was his mother, who kept house for him, and was one of the dearest old ladies in the world. She was a Quakeress, and did not at all approve of her son's occupation. As she could not change it, however, she made the best use of the opportunities for doing good afforded by his position, and many a prisoner in that jail found occasion to bless the sheriff's mother. She visited them all, did what she could for their comfort, and talked with them so earnestly, at the same time so kindly and with such ready sympathy, that several cases of complete reformation could be traced directly to her influence. Now her interest was quickly aroused by her son's account of the youthful prisoner just delivered into his keeping, and she sighed deeply over the story of his wickedness.

"Is it certain that he did all these things, Robert?" she asked at length.

"Oh, I guess there is no doubt of it. He was caught almost in the very act," answered the sheriff, carelessly.

"And thee says he is young?"

"Yes, hardly more than a boy."

"Does thee think he has had any breakfast?"

"Probably not; but I'll carry him some after I've been out and fed the cattle," answered her son, who was a farmer as well as a sheriff.

"Is thee willing I should take it to him?"

"Certainly, if you want to, only be very careful about locking everything securely after you," replied the sheriff, who was accustomed to requests of this kind. "I don't know why you should trouble yourself about him though, I'll feed him directly."

"Why should we ever trouble ourselves, Robert, about those who are strangers, or sick, or in prison? Besides, perhaps the poor lad has no mother, while just now he must sorely feel the need of one."

Thus it happened that a few minutes later Rod Blake was startled from his unhappy reverie by the appearance of an old lady in a dove-colored dress, a snowy cap and kerchief, in front of his door. As she unlocked it and stepped inside, he saw that she bore in her hands a tray on which a substantial breakfast was neatly arranged. The lad sprang to his feet, but faint from hunger and exhaustion as he was, he cast only one glance at the tempting tray. Then he gazed earnestly into the face of his visitor.

Setting the tray down on a stool, for there was no table in the cell, the old lady said: "I thought thee might be hungry my poor lad, and so have brought thee a bit of breakfast."

"Oh, madam! Don't you know me? Don't you remember me?" cried Rod eagerly.

Although startled by the boy's vehemence, the old lady adjusted her spectacles and regarded him carefully. "I can't say that I do," she said at length, in a troubled tone. "And yet thy face bears a certain look of familiarity. Where have I ever seen thee before?"

"Don't you remember one morning a few weeks ago when you were in a railroad station, and dropped your purse, and I picked it up, and you gave me a quarter for seeing you safely on the train? Don't you? I'm sure you must remember."

The old lady was nervously wiping her spectacles. As she again adjusted them and gazed keenly at the boy, a flash of recognition lighted her face and she exclaimed, "Of course I do! Of course I do! Thee is that same honest lad who restored every cent of the money that but for thee I might have lost! But what does it all mean? And how came thee here in this terrible place?"

Rod was only too thankful to have a listener at once so interested and sympathetic as this one. Forgetful of his hunger and the waiting breakfast beside him, he at once began the relating of his adventures, from the time of first meeting with the dear old lady down to the present moment. It was a long story and was so frequently interrupted by questions that its telling occupied nearly an hour.

At its conclusion the old lady, who was at once smiling and tearful, bent over and kissed the boy on his forehead, saying:

"Bless thee, lad! I believe every word of thy tale, for thee has an honest face, and an honest tongue, as well as a brave heart. Thee has certainly been cruelly rewarded for doing thy duty. Never mind, thy troubles are now ended, for my son shall quickly summons the friends who will not only prove thy innocence and release thee from this place, but must reward thy honest bravery. First, though, thee must eat thy breakfast and I must go to fetch a cup of hot coffee, for this has become cold while we talked."

So saying the old lady bustled away with a reassuring little nod and a cheery smile that to poor Rod was like a gleam of sunlight shining into a dark place. As she went, the old lady not only left his cell door unlocked but wide open for she had privately decided that the young prisoner should not be locked in again if she could prevent it.

CHAPTER XXVII.
THE SHERIFF IS INTERVIEWED.

While this pleasant recognition of old acquaintances was taking place in the jail, the sheriff was sitting in his office and submitting to be interviewed by a young man who had introduced himself as a reporter from one of the great New York dailies. He was a pleasant young man, very fluent of speech, and he treated the sheriff with a flattering deference. He explained that while in the village on other business he had incidentally heard of the important arrest made that morning and thought that if the sheriff would kindly give him a few particulars he might collect material for a good story. Pleased with the idea of having his name appear in a New York paper the sheriff readily acceded to this request and gave his visitor all the information he possessed. The young man was so interested, and took such copious notes of everything the sheriff said, that the latter was finally induced to relax somewhat of his customary caution, and take from his safe the leather bag that had been captured on the person of the alleged horse-thief. The sheriff had opened this bag when he first received it, and had glanced at its contents, of which he intended to make a careful inventory at his first leisure moment. As this had not yet arrived, he was still ignorant of what the bag really contained. He knew, however, that its contents must be of great value and produced it to prove to the reporter that the young prisoner whom they were discussing was something more than a mere horse-thief.

While the sheriff was still fumbling with the spring-catch of the bag, and before he had opened it, there came the sounds of a fall just outside the door, a crash of breaking china, and a cry in his mother's voice. Forgetful of all else, the man dropped the bag, sprang to the door, and disappeared in the hall beyond, leaving his visitor alone. In less than two minutes he returned, saying that his mother had slipped and fallen on the lowest step of the stairway she was descending. She had broken a cup and saucer, but was herself unhurt, for which he was deeply grateful. As the sheriff made this brief explanation, he cast a relieved glance at the leather bag that still lay on the floor where he had dropped it, and at some distance from the chair in which the young man was sitting.

Again he took up the bag to open it, and again he was interrupted. This time the interruption came in the shape of a messenger from the telegraph office, bringing the startling news of the recent train robbery and the daring escape of its perpetrator. The sheriff first read this despatch through to himself, and then handed it to his visitor, who had watched his face with eager interest while he read it. The moment he had glanced through the despatch, the young man started to his feet, exclaiming that such an important bit of news as that would materially alter his plans. Then he begged the sheriff to excuse him while he ran down to the telegraph office, and asked his paper for permission to remain there a few days longer. He said that he should like nothing better than a chance to assist in the capture of this desperate train robber, which he had no doubt would be speedily effected by the sheriff. He also promised to call again very shortly for further information, provided his paper gave him permission to remain.

The sheriff was not at all sorry to have his visitor depart, as the despatch just received had given new direction to his thoughts, and he was wondering if there could be any connection between the train robber, the young horse-thief, and the bag of valuables that lay unopened on his desk. He glanced curiously at it, and determined to make a thorough examination of its contents as soon as he had written and sent off several despatches containing his suspicions, asking for further information and requesting the presence at the jail of such persons as would be able to identify the train robber.

As he finished these, his mother, who had been preparing a fresh cup of coffee for Rod, entered the office full of her discovery in connection with the young prisoner and of the startling information he had given her. She would have come sooner but for the presence of her son's visitor, before whom she did not care to divulge her news.

Although the sheriff listened with interest to all she had to say, he expressed a belief that the young prisoner had taken advantage of her kindly nature, to work upon her sympathies with a plausible but easily concocted story.

"But I tell thee, Robert, I recognize the lad as the same who helped me on the train the last time I went to York."

"That may be, and still he may be a bad one."

"Never, with such a face! It is as honest as thine, Robert. Of that I am certain, and if thee will only talk with him, I am convinced thee will think as I do. Nor will thee relock the door that I left open?"

"What!" exclaimed the sheriff; "you haven't left his cell-door unlocked, mother, after the strict charges I gave you concerning that very thing?"

"Yes, I have, Robert," answered the old lady, calmly; "and but for the others I would have left the corridor-door unlocked also. I was mindful of them, though, and of thy reputation."

"I'm thankful you had that much common-sense," muttered her son; "and now, with your permission, I will take that cup of coffee, which I suppose you intend for your young ***protege***, up to him myself."

"And thee'll speak gently with him?"

"Oh, yes. I'll talk to him like a Dutch uncle."

Thus it happened that when the door at the end of the jail corridor was swung heavily back on its massive hinges, and Rod Blake, who had been gazing from one of the corridor windows, looked eagerly toward it, he was confronted by the stern face of the sheriff instead of the placidly sweet one of the old lady, whom he expected to see.

"What are you doing out here, sir? Get back into your cell at once!" commanded the sheriff in an angry tone.

"Oh, sir! please don't lock me in there again. It doesn't seem as though I could stand it," pleaded Rod.

The sheriff looked searchingly at the lad. His face was certainly a very honest one, and to one old lady at least he had been kindly considerate. At the thought of the ready help extended by this lad to his own dearly-loved mother in the time of her perplexity, the harsh words that the sheriff had meditated faded from his mind, and instead of uttering them he said:

"Very well; I will leave your cell-door open, if you will give me your promise not to attempt an escape."

And Rod promised.

CHAPTER XXVIII.
LIGHT DAWNS UPON THE SITUATION.

On leaving Rodman the sheriff was decidedly perplexed. His prisoner's honest face had made a decided impression upon him, and he had great confidence in his mother's judgment concerning such cases, though he was careful never to admit this to her. At the same time all the circumstances pointed so strongly to the lad's guilt that, as he reviewed them there hardly seemed a doubt of it. It is a peculiarity of sheriffs and jailers to regard a prisoner as guilty until he has been proved innocent. Nevertheless this sheriff gave his mother permission to visit Rod as often as she liked; only charging her to lock the corridor-door both upon entering and leaving the jail. So the dear old lady again toiled up the steep stairway, this time laden with books and papers. She found the tired lad stretched on his hard pallet and fast asleep, so she tiptoed softly away again without wakening him.

While the young prisoner was thus forgetting his troubles, and storing up new strength with which to meet them, the sheriff was scouring the village and its vicinity for traces of any stranger who might be the train robber. But strangers were scarce in Center that day and the only one he could hear of was the reporter who had interviewed him that morning. He had gone directly to the telegraph office where he had sent off the despatch of which he had spoken, to the New York paper he claimed to represent. In it he had requested an answer to be sent to Millbank, and he had subsequently engaged a livery team with which he declared his intention of driving to that place.

Center, though not on the New York and Western railway, was on another that approached the former more closely at this point than at any other. To facilitate an exchange of freight a short connecting link had been built by both roads between Center and Millbank. Over this no regular trains were run, but all the transfer business was conducted by specials controlled by operators at either end of the branch. Consequently the few travellers between the two places waited until a train happened along or, if they were in a hurry, engaged a team as the reporter had done.

Soon after noon the owner of Juniper, the stolen horse, accompanied by the thick-headed young farm hand from whom the animal had been taken, appeared at the jail in answer to the sheriff's request for his presence. These visitors were at once taken to Rod's cell, where the young prisoner greatly refreshed by his nap, sat reading one of the books left by the dear old lady. His face lighted with a glad recognition at sight of Juniper's owner, and at the same moment that gentleman exclaimed:

"Why, sheriff, this can't be the horse-thief! I know this lad. That is I engaged him not long since to bring that very horse up here to my brother's place where I am now visiting. You remember me, don't you, young man?"

"Of course I do so, sir, and I am ever so glad to see some one who knew me before all these horrid happenings. Now if you will only make that fellow explain why he said I was the one who threatened to shoot him, and stole Juniper from him, when he knows he never set eyes on me before I was arrested, I shall be ever so much obliged."

"How is this, sir?" inquired the gentleman, turning sharply upon the young farm hand behind him. "Didn't you tell me you were willing to take oath that the lad whom you caused to be arrested and the horse-thief were one and the same person?"

"Y-e-e-s, s-i-r," hesitated the thick head.

"Are you willing to swear to the same thing now?"

"N-n-o, your honor,--that is, not hexactly. Someway he don't look the same now as he did then."

"Then you don't think he is the person who took the horse from you?"

"No, sir, I can't rightly say as I do now, seeing as the man with the pistols was bigger every way than this one. If 'e 'adn't been 'e wouldn't got the 'orse so heasy,

I can tell you, sir. Besides it was so hearly that the light was dim an' I didn't see 'is face good anyway. But when we caught him 'e 'ad the 'orse an' the bag an' the pistols."

"When you caught who?"

"The 'orse-thief. I mean this young man."

"And you recognized him then?"

"Yes, sir, I knowed 'im by the bag, an' the 'orse."

"But you say he was a much larger man than this one."

"Oh, yes, sir! He was more 'n six foot an' as big across the shoulders as two of 'im."

Rod could not help smiling at this, as he recalled the slight figure of the train robber who had appropriated Juniper to his own use.

"This is evidently a badly-mixed case of mistaken identity," said the gentleman, turning to the sheriff, "and I most certainly shall not prefer any charge against this lad. Why, in connection with that same horse he recently performed one of the pluckiest actions I ever heard of." Here the speaker narrated the story of Rod's struggle with Juniper in utter darkness and within the narrow limits of a closed box-car.

At its conclusion, the sheriff who was a great admirer of personal bravery, extended his hand to Rod, saying: "I believe you to be the honest lad you claim to be, and an almighty plucky one as well. As such I want to shake hands with you. I must also state that as this gentleman refuses to enter a complaint against you I can no longer hold you prisoner. In fact I am somewhat doubtful whether I have done right in detaining you as long as I have without a warrant. Still, I want you to remain with us a few hours more, or until the arrival of certain parties for whom I have sent to come and identify the train robber."

"Meaning me?" asked Rod, with a smile. He could afford to smile now. In fact he was inclined to laugh and shout for joy over the favorable turn his fortunes appeared to be taking.

"Yes, meaning you," replied the sheriff good-humoredly. "And to show how fully persuaded I am that you are the train robber, I hereby invite you to accompany us down-stairs in the full exercise of your freedom and become the honored guest of my dear mother for whom you recently performed so kindly a service. She told me of that at the time, and I am aware now, that I have not really doubted that you were what you claimed to be, since she recognized you as the one who then befriended her. I tell you, lad, it always pays in one way or another, to extend a helping hand to grandfathers and grandmothers, and to remember that we shall probably be in need of like assistance ourselves some day."

CHAPTER XXIX.
AN ARRIVAL OF FRIENDS AND ENEMIES.

Thus it happened that although Rod had eaten his breakfast that morning in a prison cell he ate his dinner in the pleasant dining-room of the sheriff's house with that gentleman, the dear old lady, and Juniper's owner, for company. It was a very happy meal, in spite of the fact that the real train robber was still at large, and as its conversation was mostly devoted to the recent occurrences in which Rod had been so prominent an actor, his cheeks were kept in a steady glow by the praises bestowed upon him.

Directly after dinner Juniper's owner took his departure and soon afterwards a special train arrived from Millbank. It consisted of a locomotive and a single passenger coach in which were a number of New York and Western railroad men. They came in answer to the sheriff's request for witnesses who might identify the train robber. Among these new arrivals were Snyder Appleby who had been sent from New York by Superintendent Hill to investigate the affair, Conductor Tobin who, after taking the Express Special to the end of his run, had been ordered back to Millbank for this purpose, his other brakeman who had hurried ahead at the first opportunity from the station at which he had been left, the fireman of the locomotive with which Rod had chased the robber, and several others.

As this party was ushered into the sheriff's private office its members started with amazement at the sight of Rod Blake sitting there as calmly, as though perfectly at home and waiting to receive them.

Upon their entrance he sprang to his feet filled with a surprise equal to their own, for the sheriff had not told him of their coming.

"Well, sir! What are you doing here?" demanded Snyder Appleby, who was the first to recover from his surprise, and who was filled with a sense of his own importance in this affair.

"I am visiting my friend, the sheriff," answered Rod, at once resenting the other's tone and air.

"Oh, you are! And may I ask by what right you, a mere brakeman in our employ, took it upon yourself to desert your post of duty, run off with one of our engines, endanger the traffic of the line and then unaccountably disappear as you did last night or rather early this morning?"

"You may ask as much as you please," answered Rod, "but I shall refuse to answer any of your questions until I know by what authority you ask them." The young brakeman spoke quietly, but the nature of his feelings was betrayed by the hot flush that sprang to his cheeks.

"You'll find out before I'm through with you," cried Snyder savagely. "Mr. Sheriff I order you to place this fellow under arrest."

"Upon what charge?" asked the sheriff. "Is he the train robber?"

"Of course not," was the reply, "but he is a thief all the same. He is one of our brakemen and ran off with a locomotive."

"What did he do with it?" asked the sheriff, with an air of interest.

"Left it standing on the track."

"Oh, I didn't know but what he carried it off with him. Did he leave it alone and unguarded?"

Snyder was compelled to admit that the engine had been left in charge of its regular firemen; but still claimed that the young brakeman had committed a crime for which he ought to be arrested.

"I suppose you want me to arrest that fireman too?" suggested the sheriff.

"Oh, no. It was his duty to accompany the engine."

"But why didn't he refuse to allow it to move?"

"He was forced to submit by threats of personal injury made by this brakeman fellow. Isn't that so?" asked Snyder, and the fireman nodded an assent.

The sheriff smiled as he glanced first at the burly form of the fireman and then at Rod's comparatively slight figure. "Can any of these men identify this alleged locomotive thief?" he asked.

"Certainly they can. Tobin, tell the sheriff what you know of him."

Blazing with indignation at the injustice and meanness of Snyder's absurd charge against his favorite brakeman, Conductor Tobin answered promptly: "I know him to be one of the best brakemen on the road, although he is the youngest. He is one of the pluckiest too and as honest as he is plucky. I'll own he might have made a mistake in going off with that engine; but all the same it was a brave thing to do and I am certain he thought he was on the right track."

"Do you know him too?" asked the sheriff of the other brakeman.

"Yes, sir. I am proud to say I do and in regard to what I think of him Conductor Tobin's words exactly express my sentiments."

"Do you also know him?" was asked of the fireman.

"Yes, I know him to be the young rascal who ran me twice into such a storm of bullets from the train robber's pistols that it's a living wonder I'm not full of holes at this blessed minute."

"What else did he do?"

"What else? Why, he jumped from the engine while she was running a good twenty mile an hour, and started off like the blamed young lunatic he is to chase after the train robber afoot. Wanted me to go with him too, but I gave him to understand I wasn't such a fool as to go hunting any more interviews with them pistols. No, sir; I stuck where I belonged and if he'd done the same he wouldn't be in the fix he's in now."

"And yet," said the sheriff, quietly, "this 'blamed young lunatic,' as you call him, succeeded in overtaking that train robber after all. He also managed to relieve him of his pistols you seem to have dreaded so greatly, recover the valuable property that had been stolen from the express car, and also a fine horse that the robber had just appropriated to his own use. On the whole gentleman, I don't think I'd better arrest him, do you?"

CHAPTER XXX.
WHERE ARE THE DIAMONDS?

"Yes, sir. I think he ought to be arrested," said Snyder Appleby in reply to the sheriff's question, "and if you refuse to perform that duty I shall take it upon myself to arrest him in the name of the New York and Western Railway Company of which I am the representative here. I shall also take him back with me to the city where he will be dealt with according to his desserts by the proper authorities." Then turning to the members of his own party the self-important young secretary added: "In the meantime I order you two men to guard this fellow and see that he does not escape, as you value your positions on the road."

"You needn't trouble yourself, Snyder, nor them either," said Rod indignantly, "for I sha'n't require watching. I am perfectly willing to go to New York with you, and submit my case to the proper authorities. In fact I propose to do that at any rate. At the same time I want you to understand that I don't do this in obedience to any orders from you, nor will I be arrested by you."

"Oh, that's all right," replied Snyder, carelessly. "So long as we get you there I don't care how it is done. Now, Mr. Sheriff," he continued, "we have already wasted too much time and if you will take us to see the bold train robber whom you say this boy captured single-handed and alone, we will finish our business here and be off."

"I didn't say that he captured the train robber," replied the sheriff. "I stated that he overtook him, relieved him of his pistols, and recovered the stolen property; but I am quite certain that I said nothing regarding the capture of the robber."

"Where is he now?" asked Snyder.

"I don't know. This lad left him lying senseless in the road, where he had been flung by a stolen horse, and went for assistance. Being mistaken for the person who had appropriated the horse he was brought here. In the meantime the train robber recovered his senses and made good his escape. That is, I suppose he did."

"Then why did you telegraph that you had the train robber in custody, and bring us here to identify him?" demanded Snyder sharply.

"I didn't," answered the sheriff, with a provoking smile, for he was finding great pleasure in quizzing this pompously arbitrary young man. "I merely sent for a few persons who could identify the train robber to come and prove that this lad was not he. This you have kindly done to my entire satisfaction."

"What!" exclaimed Snyder. "Did you suspect Rod, I mean this brakeman, of being the train robber?"

"I must confess that I did entertain such a suspicion, and for so doing I humbly beg Mr. Blake's pardon," replied the sheriff.

"It wouldn't surprise me if he should prove to be connected with it, after all, for I believe him to be fully capable of such things," sneered Snyder.

At this cruel remark there arose such a general murmur of indignation, and the expression of Rod's face became so ominous that the speaker hastened to create a diversion of interest by asking the sheriff what had been done with the valuables recovered from the robber.

"They are in my safe."

"You will please hand them over to me."

"I shall do nothing of the kind," retorted the sheriff, as he drew the stout leather bag from its place of security. "I shall hand this bag, with all its contents, to the brave lad who recovered it, and entrust him with its safe delivery to those authorized to receive it."

So saying, the sheriff handed the bag to Rod.

Snyder turned pale with rage, and snatching an unsealed letter from his pocket, he flung it on the table, exclaiming angrily: "There is my authority for conducting this business and for receiving such of the stolen property as may be recovered. If you fail to honor it I will have you indicted for conspiracy."

"Indeed!" said the sheriff, contemptuously. "That would certainly be a most interesting proceeding--for you." Then to Rod, to whom he had already handed the bag, he said: "If you decide to deliver this property to that young man, Mr. Blake, I would advise you to examine carefully the contents of the bag in presence of these witnesses and demand an itemized receipt for them."

"Thank you, I will," replied Rod, emptying the contents of the bag on the table as he spoke.

There was a subdued exclamation from the railroad men at the sight of the wealth thus displayed in packages of bills and rolls of coin. Rodman requested the sheriff to call off the amount contained in each of these while he made out the list. At the same time Snyder drew from his pocket a similar list of the property reported to be missing from the express messenger's safe.

When Rod's list was completed, Snyder, who had carefully checked off its items on his own, said: "That's all right so far as it goes, but where are the diamonds?"

"What diamonds?" asked Rod and the sheriff together.

"The set of diamond jewelry valued at seven thousand five hundred dollars, in a morocco case, that has been missing ever since the robbery of the express car," was the answer.

"I know nothing of it," said Rod.

"This is the first I have heard of any diamonds," remarked the sheriff.

"Has the bag been out of your possession since the arrest of this--person?" asked Snyder, hesitating for a word that should express his feelings toward the lad who had once beaten him in a race, but who was now so completely in his power.

"No, sir, it has not," promptly replied the sheriff.

"You have opened it before this, of course?"

"Yes, I glanced at its contents when it was first placed in my keeping, but made no examination of them, as I should have done had not other important matters claimed my attention."

"How long was the bag in your possession?" asked Snyder, turning to Rod.

"About half an hour, but----"

"Was any one with you during that half hour?" interrupted the questioner.

"No; but as I was going to say----"

"That is sufficient. I don't care to hear what you were going to say. Others may listen to that if they choose when the proper time comes. What I have to say regarding this business is, that in view of this new development I am more than ever desirous of delivering you into the hands of the proper authorities in New York. I would also suggest that your short and brilliant career as a railroader has come to a disgraceful end more quickly than even I suspected it would."

"Do you mean to say that you think I stole those diamonds?" demanded Rod, hotly.

"Oh, no," answered Snyder. "I don't say anything about it. The circumstances of the case speak so plainly for themselves that my testimony would be superfluous. Now, Mr. Sheriff, as our business here seems to be concluded, I think we will bid you good-by and be moving along."

"You needn't bid me good-by yet," responded the sheriff, "for I have decided to go with you."

"I doubt if I shall be able to find room for you in my special car," said Snyder, who for several reasons was not desirous of the sheriff's company.

"Very well. Then you will be obliged to dispense with Mr. Blake's company also, for in view of the recent developments in this case I feel that I ought not to lose sight of him just yet."

CHAPTER XXXI.
ONE HUNDRED MILES AN HOUR!

The sheriff's concluding argument at once prevailed. Snyder was so eager to witness his rival's humiliation and to hear the Superintendent pronounce his sentence of dismissal from the company's employ, that he would have sacrificed much of his own dignity rather than forego that triumph. As matters now stood he could not see how Rod, even though he should not be convicted of stealing the missing diamonds, could clear himself from the suspicion of having done so.

Neither could poor Rod see how it was to be accomplished. For mile after mile of that long ride back toward New York he sat in silence, puzzling over the situation. In spite of the attempts of the sheriff and Conductor Tobin to cheer him up, he grew more and more despondent at the prospect of having to go through life as one who is suspected. It was even worse than being locked into a prison cell, for he had known that could not last long, while this new trouble seemed interminable.

The lad's sorrowful reflections were interrupted by an ejaculation from the sheriff who sat beside him. On that gentleman's knee lay an open watch, at which he had been staring intently and in silence for some time. He had also done some figuring on a pad of paper. Finally he uttered a prolonged "Wh-e-w!"

Both Rod and Conductor Tobin looked at him inquiringly.

"Do you know," he said, "that we have just covered a mile in forty-two seconds, and that we are travelling at the rate of eighty-five miles an hour?"

"I shouldn't be surprised," replied Conductor Tobin, quietly; "I heard Mr. Appleby tell the engineman at the last stop that if better time wasn't made pretty soon he'd go into the cab himself and show 'em how to do it. The idea of his talking that way to an old driver like Newman. Why, I don't believe he knows the difference between a throttle and an injector. A pretty figure he'd cut in a cab! Newman didn't answer him a word, only gave him a queer kind of a look. Now he's hitting her up for all she's worth, though, and, judging from appearances, Mr. Appleby wishes he'd held his tongue."

Snyder certainly was very pale, and was clutching the arms of his seat as though to keep himself from being flung to the floor during the frightful lurchings of the car as it spun around curves.

"But isn't it middling dangerous to run so fast?" asked the sheriff, as the terrific speed seemed to increase.

"Not so very," answered the Conductor. "I don't consider that there is any more danger at a high rate of speed than there is at forty or fifty miles an hour! If we were to strike a man, a cow, a wagon, or even a pile of ties while going at this rate we'd fling the obstacle to one side like a straw and pay no more attention to it. If we were only doing fifteen or twenty miles though, instead of between eighty and ninety, any one of these things would be apt to throw us off the track. I tell you, gentleman, old man Newman is making things hum though! You see he has got number 385, one of the new compound engines. He claims that she can do one hundred miles an hour just as well as not, and that he is the man to get it out of her. He says he can stand it if she can. He made her do a mile in 39-1/4 seconds on her trial trip, and claims that about a month ago when he was hauling the grease wagon[1] she did 4-1/10 miles in 2-1/2 minutes, which is at the rate of 98.4 miles an hour.[2] His fireman backs him up, and says he held the stop-watch between stations. The paymaster was so nearly scared to death that time that Newman was warned never to try for his hundred-mile record again without special orders. Now I suppose he considers that he has received them and is making the most of his chance."

[1] Pay-car.

[2] This time has actually been made by an American locomotive on an American railroad.--K. M.

"It's awful!" gasped Snyder, who had drawn near enough to the group to over-hear the last of Conductor Tobin's remarks. "The man must be crazy. Isn't there some way of making him slow down?"

"Not if he is crazy, as you suggest, sir," replied Conductor Tobin, with a sly twinkle in his eyes. "It would only make matters worse to interfere with him now, and all we can do is to hope for the best."

"It's glorious!" shouted Rod, forgetting all his troubles in the exhilaration of this wild ride. "It's glorious! And I only hope he'll make it. Do you really think a hundred miles an hour is within the possibilities, Mr. Tobin?"

"Certainly I do," answered the Conductor. "It not only can be done, but will be, very soon. I haven't any doubt but what by the time the Columbian Exposition opens we shall have regular passenger trains running at that rate over some stretches of our best roads, such as the Pennsylvania, the Reading, the New York Central and this one. Moreover, when electricity comes into general use as a motive power I shall expect to travel at a greater speed even than that. Why, they are building an electric road now on an air line between Chicago and St. Louis, on which they expect to make a hundred miles an hour as a regular thing."

"I hope I shall have a chance to travel on it," said Rod.

"I have heard of another road," continued Conductor Tobin, "now being built somewhere in Europe, Austria I believe, over which they propose to run trains at the rate of one hundred and twenty-five miles an hour."

Here the conversation was interrupted by Snyder Appleby, who, in a frenzy of terror that he could no longer control, shouted "Stop him! Stop him! I order you to stop him at once!"

"All right, sir, I'll try," answered Conductor Tobin, with a scornful smile on his face. Just as he lifted his hand to the bell-cord there came a shriek from the locomotive whistle. It was instantly followed by such a powerful application of brakes that the car in which our friends were seated quivered in every joint and seemed as though about to be wrenched in pieces.

As the special finally came to a halt, and its occupants rushed out to discover the cause of its violent stoppage, they found the hissing monster, that had drawn them with such fearful velocity, standing trembling and panting within a few feet of one of the most complete and terrible wrecks any of them had ever seen.

CHAPTER XXXII.
SNATCHING VICTORY FROM DEFEAT.

The wreck by which the terrific speed of the special had been so suddenly checked was one of those that may happen at any time even on the best and most carefully-managed of railroads. The through freight, of which ex-Brakeman Joe was now conductor, had made its run safely and without incident to a point within twenty miles of New York. It was jogging along at its usual rate of speed when suddenly and without the slightest warning an axle under a "foreign" car, near the rear of the train, snapped in two. In an instant the car leaped from the rails and across the west-bound tracks, dragging the rear end of the freight, including the caboose, after it. Before the dazed train-hands could realize what was happening, the heavy locomotive of a west-bound freight that was passing the east-bound train at that moment crashed into the wreck. It struck a tank-car filled with oil. Like a flash of lightning a vast column of fire shot high in the air and billows of flame were roaring in every direction. These leaped from one to another of the derailed cars, until a dozen belonging to both trains, as well as the west-bound locomotive, were enveloped in their cruel embrace.

Conductor Joe escaped somehow, but he was bruised, shaken, and stunned by the suddenness and awfulness of the catastrophe. In spite of his bewilderment, however, his years of training as a brakeman were not forgotten. Casting but a single glance at the blazing wreck, he turned and ran back along the east-bound track. He was no coward running away from duty and responsibility, though almost any one who saw him just then might have deemed him one. No, indeed! He was doing what none but a faithful and experienced railroad man would have thought of doing under the circumstances; doing his best to avert further calamity by warning approaching trains from the west of the danger before them. He ran half a mile and then placed the torpedoes, which, with a brakeman's instinct, he still carried in his pocket.

Bang-bang! BANG! Engineman Newman, driving locomotive number 385 at nearer one hundred miles an hour than it had ever gone before, heard the sharp reports above the rattling roar of his train, and realized their dread significance. It was a close call, and only cool-headed promptness could have checked the tremendous speed of that on-rushing train in the few seconds allowed for the purpose. As it was, 385's paint was blistering in the intense heat from the oil flames as it came to a halt and then slowly backed to a place of safety.

Conductor Joe had already returned to the scene of the wreck and was sending out other men with torpedoes and flags in both directions. Then he joined the brave fellows who were fighting for the lives of those still imprisoned in the wrecked caboose. Among these were Rod Blake, Conductor Tobin, and the sheriff. Snyder Appleby had turned sick at the heartrending sights and sounds to be seen and heard on all sides, and had gone back to his car to escape them. He did not believe a soul could be saved, and he had not the nerve to listen to the pitiful cries of those whom he considered doomed to a certain destruction.

In thus accepting defeat without a struggle, Snyder exhibited the worst form of cowardice, and if the world were made up of such as he, there would be no victories to record. But it is not. It not only contains those who will fight against overwhelming odds, but others who never know that they are beaten, and where indomitable wills often snatch victory from what appears to be defeat. General Grant was one of these, and Rod Blake was made of the same stuff.

Again and again he and those with him plunged into the stifling smoke to battle with the fierce flames in their stronghold. They smothered them with clods of earth and buckets of sand. They cut away the blazing woodwork with keen-edged wrecking axes torn from their racks in the uninjured caboose and in Snyder Appleby's special car. One by one they released and dragged out the victims, of whom the fire had been so certain, until none was left, and a splendid victory had been snatched from what had promised to be a certain defeat.

There was a farm-house not far away, to which the victims of the disaster were tenderly borne. Here, too, came their rescuers, scorched, blackened, and exhausted; but forgetful of their own plight in their desire to further relieve the sufferings of those for whom they had done such brave battle. In one of the wounded men Rod Blake was especially interested, for the young brakeman had fought on with a stubborn determination to save him after the others had declared it to be impossible. The man had been a passenger in the caboose of the through freight, and was so crushed and held by the shattered timbers of the car that, though the rescuing party reached his side, they were unable to drag him out. A burst of flame drove them back and forced them to rush into the open air to save their own lives. Above the roar of the fire they could distinguish his piteous cries, and this was more than Rod could stand. With a wet cloth over his mouth and axe in hand he dashed back into the furnace. He was gone before the others knew what he was about to attempt, and now they listened with bated breath to the sound of rapid blows coming from behind the impenetrable veil of swirling smoke. As it eddied upward and was lifted for an instant they caught sight of him, and rushing to the spot, they dragged him out, with his arms tightly clasped about the helpless form he had succeeded in releasing from its fiery prison.

At that moment the young brakeman presented a sorry picture, blackened beyond recognition by his dearest friends, scorched, and with clothing hanging in charred shreds. By some miracle he was so far uninjured that a few dashes of cold water gave him strength to walk, supported by Conductor Tobin, to the farm-house, whither the others bore the unconscious man whom he had saved. The lad wished to help minister to the needs of the sufferer, but those who had cheered his act of successful bravery now insisted upon his taking absolute rest. So they made him lie down in a dimly-lighted room, where the sheriff sat beside him, and, big rough man that he was, soothed the exhausted lad with such tender gentleness, that after awhile the latter fell asleep. When this happened and the sheriff stole quietly out to where the others were assembled, he said emphatically:

"Gentlemen, I am prouder to know that young fellow than I would be of the friendship of a president."

CHAPTER XXXIII.
A WRECKING TRAIN.

While Rod lay in a dreamless sleep, which is the best and safest of remedies for every ill, mental or physical, that human flesh is heir to, a wrecking train arrived from New York. With it came a doctor, who was at once taken to the farm-house. He first looked at the sleeping lad, but would not allow him to be wakened, then he turned his attention to the victims of the disaster, whose poor maimed bodies were so sadly in need of his soothing skill.

During the long hours of the night, while the doctor was busy with his human wrecks, the gang of experienced workmen who had come by the same train, was rapidly clearing the wreck of cars from the tracks and putting them in order for a speedy resumption of traffic. The wrecking train to which they belonged was made up of a powerful locomotive and three cars. The first of these was an immensely strong and solid flat, supporting a small derrick, which was at the same time so powerful as to be capable of lifting enormous weights. Besides the derrick and its belongings the flat carried only a few spare car trucks.

Next to it came a box-car, filled with timber ends for blocking, hawsers, chains, ropes, huge single-, double-, and treble-blocks, iron clamps, rods and bolts, frogs, sections of rail, heavy tarpaulins for the protection of valuable freight, and a multitude of other like supplies, all so neatly arranged as to be instantly available.

Last, and most interesting of all, came the tool-car, which was divided by partitions into three rooms. Of these, the main one was used by the members of the wrecking gang as a living-room, and was provided with bunks, a cooking-stove and utensils, and a pantry, well stocked with flour, coffee, tea, and canned provisions. The smaller of the two end rooms contained a desk, table, chairs, stationery and electrical supplies. It was used by the foreman of the wrecking gang, as an office in which to write his reports, and by the telegraph operator, who always accompanies a train of this description. This operator's first duty is to connect an instrument in his movable office with the railroad wire, which is one of the many strung on poles beside the track. From the temporary station thus established he is in constant communication with headquarters, to which he sends all possible information concerning the wreck, and from which he receives orders.

In the tool-room at the other end of this car was kept everything that experience could suggest or ingenuity devise for handling and removing wrecked cars, freight, or locomotives. Along the sides were ranged a score or so of jack-screws, some of them powerful enough to lift a twenty-ton weight, though worked by but one man. There were also wrenches, axes, saws, hammers of all sizes, crowbars, torches, lanterns, drills, chisels, files, and, in fact, every conceivable tool that might be of use in an emergency.

In less than three hours after the arrival of the wrecking train at the scene of the accident on the New York and Western road, the disabled locomotive, which had lain on its side in the ditch, had been picked up and replaced on the track. Such of the derailed cars as were not burned or crushed beyond hope of repair had also been restored to their original positions, scattered freight had been gathered up and reloaded, all inflammable **debris** was being burned in a great heap at one side, the tracks were repaired, and so little remained to tell of the disaster, that passengers by the next day's trains looked in vain for its traces.

The first train to go through after the accident was Snyder Appleby's special. The private secretary had visited the farm-house to insist that Rod Blake should accompany him to New York; but he was met at the door by the watchful sheriff, who sternly refused to allow his sleeping charge to be awakened or in any way disturbed.

"You needn't worry yourself about him," said the sheriff. "He'll come to New York fast enough, and I'll come with him. We'll hunt the Superintendent's office as quick as we get there, and maybe you won't be so glad to see us as you think you will. That's the best I can promise you, for that young fellow isn't going to be disturbed before he gets good and ready to wake up of his own accord. Not if I can help it, and I rather think I can."

"Oh, well," replied Snyder, who in the seclusion of his car had heard nothing of Rod's brave fight. "If he is such a tender plant that his sleep can't be interrupted, I suppose I shall have to go on without him, for my time is too valuable to be wasted in waiting here any longer. But I warn you, sir, that if you don't produce the young man in our office at an early hour to-morrow morning the company will hold you personally responsible for the loss of those diamonds."

So saying, and ordering Conductor Tobin with the other witnesses to accompany him, the self-important young secretary took his departure, filled with anger against Rod Blake, the sheriff who had constituted himself the lad's champion, the wreck by which he had been delayed, and pretty nearly everything else that happened to cross his mind at that moment.

As for Rod, he slept so peacefully and soundly until long after sunrise, that when he awoke and gazed inquiringly about him, he was but little the worse for his thrilling experiences of the previous night. His first question after collecting his scattered thoughts was concerning the welfare of the man for whom he had risked so much a few hours before.

"The poor fellow died soon after midnight," replied the sheriff. "He did not suffer, for he was unconscious to the last, but in spite of that he left you a legacy, which I believe you will consider an ample reward for your brave struggle to save him. At any rate, I know it is one that you will value as long as you live."

CHAPTER XXXIV.
ROD ACCEPTS THE LEGACY.

"I sha'n't accept it," declared Rod. "I couldn't take a reward for trying to save a man's life. You couldn't yourself, sir. You know that all the money in the world wouldn't have tempted you into those flames, while you were ready enough to go on the simple chance of saving a human being from an awful death. I'm sure you must feel that way, and so you know just how I feel about it. I only wish he could have known it too, and known how willingly we tried to save him. If he only had, he wouldn't have thought of offering us a reward. Did you find out who he was?"

"Yes, I found out," answered the sheriff, with a queer little smile. "I found out, too, that he was some one whom you knew quite well and were deeply interested in."

"Some one I knew!" cried Rod, in surprise, at the same time taking a rapid mental note of all his railroad friends who might have been connected with the accident. "Who was he? Was he a railroad man?"

"No, he was not a railroad man, and I can't tell you his name, but if you feel strong enough, I should like to have you come and take a look at him."

"Of course I do," replied Rod whose curiosity was now fully aroused. "I feel almost as well as ever I did, excepting a little shaky, and with a smart here and there in the burned places."

As the two entered an adjoining room, Rod's attention was instantly attracted by the motionless form, covered with a sheet, that lay on a bed. Several persons were engaged in a low-voiced conversation at one end of the room; but at first the lad did not notice them. He was too anxious to discover which of all his friends lay there so silently, to heed aught else just then.

As he and the sheriff stepped to the side of the bed, the latter gently withdrew the covering and disclosed a peaceful face, from which every trace of grime and smoke had been tenderly removed.

Rod instantly recognized it. It was the same that he had last seen only the morning before lying by the forest roadside more than a hundred miles away. In a tone of awed amazement he exclaimed, "the train robber!"

"I think that settles it, gentlemen," said the sheriff quietly, and turning to the other occupants of the room who had gathered close behind Rod. "We thought it must be the train robber," he continued, addressing the latter "because we found the missing diamonds in a breast pocket of his coat; but we wanted your evidence to establish the fact. I have also recognized him as the alleged reporter who interviewed me yesterday morning, and who was accidentally left alone for a minute with the leather bag in my office. The moment I discovered that the diamonds were missing I suspected that he must have taken them, but thought it best to keep my suspicions to myself until I could trace him. I learned that a man answering his description had boarded the east-bound freight somewhere this side of Millbank and telegraphed Conductor Joe Miller to keep him in sight. By making use of Mr. Appleby's special I hoped to overtake and pass him before he reached New York. I thus expected to be on hand to welcome and arrest him at his journey's end, and by so doing relieve you of all suspicion of being anything but the honest plucky lad you have proved yourself. At the same time I looked forward to taking some of the conceit out of that young sprig of a secretary. That all my calculations were not upset by last night's accident was largely owing to you, for I must confess that, but for the shame of being outdone in bravery by a mere slip of a boy, I should have given up the fight to save this man long before the victory was won. Of course the evidence of his crime would have vanished with him, and we should never have known for a certainty what had become of the train robber or the diamonds. Some persons might even have continued to suspect you of being connected with their disappearance, while now your record is one that any man may well envy. Was I not right then, in saying that this poor fellow had left you a reward for your bravery that you will value so long as you live?"

"Indeed you were," answered Rod, in a low tone, "and it is a legacy that I can most gratefully accept, I wish he might have lived, though. It is terrible to think that by following him as I did I drove him to his death."

"You must not think of it in that way," said one of the other witnesses of the scene, taking the lad's hand as he spoke, and at the same time disclosing the well-known features of Mr. Hill, the Superintendent, "You must only remember that you have done your duty faithfully and splendidly. Although I should not have approved the course you took at the outset, the results fully justify all that you have done, and I am very proud to number you among the employees of our company. You have certainly graduated with honors from the ranks of brakemen, and have fairly won your promotion to any position that you feel competent to fill. It only rests with you to say what it shall be."

"If the young man would accept a position with us," interrupted another gentleman, whom Rod knew to be a superintendent of the Express Company, "we should be only too happy to offer him one, that carries with it a handsome salary and the promise of speedy promotion."

"No, indeed! You can't have him!" exclaimed Mr. Hill. "A railroad company is said to be a soulless corporation, but it has at least soul enough to appreciate and desire to retain such services as this lad has shown himself capable of rendering. He has chosen to be a railroad man, and I don't believe he is ready to switch off on any other line just yet. How is it, Blake? Have you had enough of railroading?"

"No, sir," replied Rod, earnestly. "I certainly have not. I have only had enough of it to make me desirous of continuing in it, and if you think I could make a good enough fireman, I should be very glad to take Milt Sturgis' place on number 10, and learn to run a locomotive engine under Mr. Stump."

"A fireman!" exclaimed Mr. Hill, in surprise. "Is that the height of your ambition?"

"I think it is at present, sir," replied Rod, modestly.

"But I thought you knew how to run an engine. It looked that way yesterday morning when you started off with the one belonging to the express special."

"I thought I did too, sir; but by that very trial I found that I knew just nothing at all about it. I do want to learn though, and if you haven't anyone else in view----"

"Of course you shall have the place if you want it," interrupted Mr. Hill. "Stump has already applied for you, and you should have had it even if all the events of yesterday had not happened. I must tell you though, that Joe Miller wants to resign his conductorship of the through freight to accept a position on a private car belonging to a young millionaire oil prince, and I was thinking of offering you his place."

"Thank you ever so much, sir; but if you don't mind, I would rather run on number 10."

"Very well," replied the Superintendent, "you have earned the right to do as you think best. Now, as the track is again clear, we will all go back to the city in the wrecking train, which is ready to start."

When Mr. Hill entered his office an hour later his secretary handed him a report of his investigations in the matter of the express robbery. This report cast grave suspicions upon Rod Blake as having been connected with the affair, and advised his arrest. Snyder had spent some hours in preparing this document, and now awaited with entire self complaisance the praise which he was certain would reward his efforts. What then was his amazement when his superior, after glancing through the report, deliberately tore it into fragments, which he dropped into a waste-basket. At the same time he said:

"I am pleased to be able to inform you, Mr. Appleby, that the property you describe as missing has been recovered through the agency of this very Rodman Blake. I must also warn you that the company has no employee of whose integrity and faithfulness in the performance of duty they are more assured than they are of his. As you have evidently failed to discover this in your dealings with Mr. Blake, and as you have blundered through this investigation from first to last, I shall hereafter have no use for your services outside of routine office work." Thus saying, Mr. Hill closed the door of his private office behind him, leaving Snyder overwhelmed with bewilderment and indignation.

CHAPTER XXXV.
FIRING ON NUMBER 10.

In regard to Rod Blake's new appointment, nothing more was said that day; but, sure enough, he received an order the following morning to report to the master mechanic for duty as fireman on engine number 10.

Proud enough of his promotion, the lad promptly obeyed the order; and when that same evening he climbed into the cab of number 10, as the huge machine with a full head of steam on stood ready to start out with Freight Number 73, he felt that one of his chief ambitions was in a fair way of being realized. He tried to thank Truman Stump for getting him the job; but the old engineman only answered "Nonsense, you won the place for yourself, and I'm glad enough to have such a chap as you. The only trouble is that you'll learn too quick, and be given an engine of your own, just as you are getting the hang of my ways. I won't teach you anything though, except how to fire properly, so you needn't expect it."

That is what he said. What he did was to take every opportunity for showing the young fireman the different parts of the wonderful machine on which they rode, and of explaining them to him in the clearest possible manner. He encouraged him to ask questions, often allowed him to handle the throttle for short distances, and evidently took the greatest pride in the rapid progress made by his pupil.

Since first obtaining employment on the railroad, Rod had, according to his promise, written several times to his faithful friend Dan the stable boy on his uncle's place with requests that he would keep him informed of all that took place in the village. Dan sent his answers through the station agent at Euston, and Rod had only been a fireman a few days when he received a note which read as follows:

"DEAR MR. ROD:
"They is a man here, who I don't know, but who is asking all about you. He asked me many questions, and has talk with your uncle. He may mean good or he may mean bad, I don't know which. If I find out ennything more I will let you know.
Yours respectful,

"DAN."

Rod puzzled over this note a good deal, and wondered who on earth could be making inquiries about him. If he had known that it was Brown the railroad detective, he would have wondered still more. He finally decided that, as he was not conscious of having done anything wrong, he had no cause for worry. So he dismissed the affair, and devoted his whole attention to learning to be a fireman.

Most people imagine it to be a very simple matter to shovel coal into a locomotive furnace, and so it is; but this is only a small part of a fireman's responsibility. He must know when to begin shovelling coal, and when to stop; when to open the blower and when to shut it off; when to keep the furnace door closed, and when to open it; how to regulate the dampers; when and how to admit water to the boiler;

when to pour oil into the lubricating cups of the cylinder valves and a dozen other places; when to ring the bell, and when and how to do a multitude of other things, every one of which is important. He must keep a constant watch of the steam-gauge, and see that its pointer does not fall below a certain mark. The water-gauge also comes in for a share of his attention. Above all, he must learn, as quickly as possible, how to start, stop, and reverse the engine, and how to apply, or throw off the air brakes, so that he can readily do any of these things in an emergency, if his engineman happens to be absent.

In acquiring all this information, and at the same time attending to his back-breaking work of shovelling coal, Rod found himself so fully and happily occupied that he could spare but few thoughts to the stranger who was inquiring about him in Euston. After a few days of life in the cab of locomotive number 10, he became so accustomed to dashing through tunnels amid a blackness so intense that he could not see a foot beyond the cab windows, to whirling around sharp curves, to rattling over slender trestles a hundred feet or more up in the air, and to rushing with undiminished speed through the darkness of storm-swept nights, when the head-lights seemed of little more value than a tallow candle, that he ceased to think of the innumerable dangers connected with his position as completely as though they had not existed.

There came a day, however, when they were recalled to his mind in a startling manner. It was late in the fall, and for a week there had been a steady down-pour of rain that filled the streams to overflowing, and soaked the earth until it seemed like a vast sponge. It made busy work for the section gangs, who had their hands more than full with landslides, undermined culverts, and overflowing ditches, and it caused enginemen to strain their eyes along the lines of wet track, with an unusual carefulness. At length the week of rain ended with a storm of terrific violence, accompanied by crashing thunder and vivid lightnings. While this storm was at its height, locomotive number 10, drawing a heavy freight, pulled in on the siding of a station to wait for the passing of a passenger special, and a regular express.

Truman Stump sat on his side of the cab, calmly smoking a short, black pipe; and his fireman stood at the other side, looking out at the storm as the special, consisting of a locomotive and two cars, rushed by without stopping. As it was passing, a ball of fire, accompanied by a rending crash of thunder, illumined the whole scene with an awful, blinding glare. For an instant Rod saw a white face pressed against one of the rear windows of the flying train. He was almost certain that it was the face of Eltje Vanderveer.

A moment later the telegraph operator of that station came running toward them, bareheaded, and coatless, through the pitiless rain. The head-light showed his face to be bloodless and horror-stricken.

"Cut loose from the train, Rod!" he cried in a voice husky and choked with a terrible dread. "True, word was just coming over the wire that the centre pier of Minkskill bridge had gone out from under the track, and for me to stop all trains, when that last bolt struck the line, and cut me off. If you can't catch that special there's no hope for it. It's the only thing left to try."

Without waiting to hear all this Rod had instantly obeyed the first order, sprung to the rear of the tender, drawn the coupling-pin, and was back in the cab in less time than it takes to write of it. Truman Stump did not utter a word; but, before the operator finished speaking, number 10 was in motion. He had barely time to leap to the ground as she gathered headway and began to spring forward on the wildest race for life or death ever run on the New York and Western road.

CHAPTER XXXVI.
THE ONLY CHANCE OF SAVING THE SPECIAL.

So well did Truman Stump and his young fireman understand each other, that, as locomotive number 10 sprang away on her race after the special, there was no ne-cessity for words between them. Only after Rod had done everything in his power to ensure a full head of steam and paused for a moment's breathing-spell, did he step up behind the engineman and ask, "What is it, True?"

"Minkskill bridge gone! We are trying to catch the special," answered the driver, briefly, without turning his head. It was enough; and Rod instantly comprehended the situation. There was a choking sensation in his throat, as he remembered the face disclosed by the lightning a few moments before, and realized the awful danger that now threatened the sunny-haired girl who had been his playmate, and was still his friend. With a desperate energy he flung open the furnace-door, and toiled to feed the roaring flames behind it. They almost licked his face in their mad leapings, as their scorching breath mingled with his. He was bathed in perspiration; and, when the front windows of the cab were forced open by the fierce pressure of the gale, he welcomed the cold blast and hissing rain that swept through it.

Number 10 had now attained a fearful speed, and rocked so violently from side to side that its occupants were obliged to brace themselves and cling to the solid framework. It was a miracle that she kept the track. At each curve, and there were many of them on this section, Rod held his breath, fully expecting the mighty mass of iron to leap from the rails and plunge headlong into the yawning blackness. But she clung to them, and the steady hand at the throttle opened it wider, and still a little wider, until the handle had passed any limit that even the old engineman had ever seen. Still the young fireman, with set teeth and nerves like steel, watched the dial on the steam-gauge, and flung coal to the raging flames behind the glowing furnace-door.

Mile after mile was passed in half the same number of minutes, and outside objects were whirled backward in one continuous, undistinguishable blur. The limb of a tree, flung to the track by the mighty wind, was caught up by the pilot and dashed against the head-light, instantly extinguishing it. So they rushed blindly on, through a blackness intensified by gleams of electric light, that every now and then ran like fiery serpents along the rails, or bathed the flying engine with its pallid flames.

They were not more than two miles from the deadly bridge when they first saw the red lights on the rear of the special. The engineman's hand clutched the whistle lever; and, high above the shriek of the storm, sounded the quick, sharp blasts of the danger signal. A moment later they swept past a glare of red fire blazing beside the track. The enginemen of the special had not understood their signal, and had thrown out a fusee to warn them of his presence immediately in front of them.

"I'll have to set you aboard, Rod," shouted Truman Stump, and the young fireman knew what he meant. He did not answer; but crawling through the broken window and along the reeling foot-board, using his strength and agility as he had never used them before, the boy made his way to the pilot of the locomotive. Crouching there, and clinging to its slippery braces, he made ready for the desperate spring that should save or lose everything.

Foot by foot, in reality very quickly, but seemingly at a laggard pace, he was borne closer and closer to the red lights, until they shone full in his face. Then, with all his energies concentrated into one mighty effort, he launched himself forward, and caught, with outstretched hands, the iron railing of the platform on which were the lights. Drawing himself up on it, he dashed into the astonished group standing in the glass-surrounded observation-room, that occupied the rear of the car, crying:

"Stop the train! Stop it for your lives!"

Prompt obedience to orders, without pausing to question them, comes so naturally to a railroad man, that President Vanderveer himself now obeyed this grimy-faced young fireman as readily as though their positions had been reversed. With a quick movement he touched a button at one side of the car, and instantly a clear-voiced electric bell, in the cab of the locomotive that was dragging his train toward destruction, rang out an imperative call for brakes. The engineman's right hand sought the little brass "air" lever as he heard the sound. With his left he shut off steam. Ten seconds later the special stood motionless, with its pilot pointing out over the Minskill bridge.

President Vanderveer had not recognized the panting, coal-begrimed, oil-stained young fireman who had so mysteriously boarded his car while it was running at full speed; but Eltje knew his voice. Now, as her father turned from the electric button to demand an explanation, he saw the girl seize the stranger's hand. "It's Rod, father! It's Rodman Blake!" she cried.

"So it is!" exclaimed the President, grasping the lad's other hand, and scanning him closely. "But what is the matter, Rodman? How came you here? Why have you stopped us, and what is the meaning of this disguise?"

A few words served to explain the situation.

Then the President, with Rod and the conductor of the special, left the car, lanterns in hand, to go ahead and discover how far they were from the treacherous bridge. As they reached the ground they were joined by Truman Stump, who had slowed the terrific speed of his locomotive at the moment of his fireman's leap from its pilot, and brought it to a standstill close behind the special. In a voice trembling with emotion the old engineman said:

"It was the finest thing I've seen done in thirty years of running, Rod, and I thank God for your nerve."

A minute later, when President Vanderveer realized the full extent of the threatened danger, and the narrowness of their escape, he again held the young fireman's hand, as he said:

"And I thank God, Rodman, not only for your nerve, but that he permitted you to be on time. A few seconds later and our run on this line would have been ended forever."

After a short consultation it was decided that the special should remain where it was, while locomotive number 10 should run back to the station, where its train still waited, bearing a message to be telegraphed to the nearest gang of bridge carpenters.

How different was that backward ride from the mad, breathless race, with all its dreadful uncertainties, that Truman Stump and Rod Blake had just made over the same track. How silent they had been then, and how they talked now. How cheerily their whistle sounded as they approached the station! How lustily Rod pulled at the bell-rope, that the glad tidings of number 10's glorious run might the sooner be guessed by the anxious watchers, who awaited their coming. What an eager throng gathered round the old locomotive as it rolled proudly up to the station. It almost seemed conscious of having performed a splendid deed. Long afterwards, in cab and caboose, or wherever the men of the N. Y. and W. road gathered, all fast time was compared with the great run made by number 10 on that memorable night.

The storm had passed and the moon was shining when the station was reached. Already men were at work repairing the telegraph line, and an hour later a bridge gang, with a train of timber-laden flats, was on its way to the Minkskill bridge. Number 10 drew this train, and Rod was delighted to have this opportunity to learn something of bridge building. He was glad, too, to escape from the praises of the railroad men; for Truman Stump insisted on telling the story of his young fireman's brave deed to each new crew as it reached the station, and they were equally determined to make a hero of him.

CHAPTER XXXVII.
INDEPENDENCE OR PRIDE

Smiler, the railroad dog, appeared on the scene with the bridge gang, though no one knew where he came from; and, quickly discovering Rod, he followed him into the cab of locomotive number 10. Here he took possession of the cushion on the fireman's side of the cab, and sat on it with a wise expression on his honest face, that said as plainly as words: "This is an important bit of work, and it is clearly my duty to superintend it." Rod was delighted to have this opportunity of introducing the dear dog to Eltje, and they became friends immediately. As for the President, Smiler not only condescended to recognize him, but treated him with quite as much cordiality as though he had been a fireman or a brakeman on a through freight.

Rod got a few hours' sleep that night after all, and in the morning he and Engineman Stump accepted an invitation to take breakfast with President Vanderveer, his daughter, and Smiler, in the President's private car. This car had just returned from the extended western trip on which it had started two months before, when Rod was seeking employment on the road. As neither Eltje nor her father had heard a word concerning him in all that time, they now plied him with questions. When he finished his story Eltje exclaimed:

"I think it is perfectly splendid, Rod, and if I were only a boy I would do just as you have done! Wouldn't you, papa?"

"I am not quite sure that I would, my dear," answered her father, with a smile. "While I heartily approve of a boy who wishes to become a railroad man, beginning at the very bottom of the ladder and working his way up, I cannot approve of his leaving his home with the slightest suspicion of a stain resting on his honor if he can possibly help it. Don't you think, Rodman," he added kindly, turning to the lad, "that the more manly course would have been to have stayed in Euston until you had solved the problem of who really did disable your cousin's bicycle?"

"I don't know but what it would," replied the young man, thoughtfully; "but it would have been an awfully hard thing to do."

"Yes, I know it would. It would have been much harder than going hungry or fighting tramps or capturing express robbers; still it seems to me that it would have been more honorable."

"But Uncle turned me out of the house."

"Did he order you to leave that very night, or did he ask you to make arrangements to do so at some future time, and promise to provide for you when you did go?"

"I believe he did say something of that kind," replied Rod, hesitatingly.

"Do you believe he would have said even that the next morning!"

"Perhaps not, sir."

"You know he wouldn't, Rodman. You know, as well as I do, that Major Appleby says a great many things on the impulse of the moment that he sincerely regrets upon reflection. He told me himself the morning I left Euston how badly he felt that you should have taken his hasty words so literally. He said that he should do everything in his power to cause you to forget them the moment you returned, as he hoped you would in a day or two. He gave Snyder instructions to use every effort to discover you in the city, where it was supposed you had gone, and provided him liberally with money to be expended in searching for you. I am surprised that Snyder has not found you out before this, especially as you are both in the employ of the same company. Didn't you know that he was private secretary to our superintendent?"

"Yes, sir; I did," replied Rod, "and----" He was about to add, "And he knows where I am"; but obeying a more generous impulse, he changed it to "and I have taken pains to avoid him."

"I am sorry for that," said the President; "for if he had only met you and delivered your uncle's message you would have been reconciled to that most impetuous but most kindly-hearted of gentlemen long ago. Now, however, you will go home with us and have a full explanation with him, will you not?"

"I think not, sir," replied Rod, with a smile. "In the first place, I can't leave Mr. Stump, here, to run number 10 without a fireman, and in the second I would a great deal rather wait until I hear directly from my uncle that he wants me. Besides, I don't want to give up being a railroad man; for, after the experience I have gained, I am more determined than ever to be one."

"It would be a great pity, sir, to have so promising a young railroader lost to the business," said Truman Stump, earnestly, "and I do hope you won't think of taking him from us."

"I should think, papa, that you would be glad to have anybody on the road who can do such splendid things as Rod can," said Eltje, warmly. "I'm sure if I were president, I'd promote him at once, and make him conductor, or master of something, instead of trying to get rid of him. Why, it's a perfect shame!"

"I've no doubt, dear, that if you were president, the road would be managed just as it should be. As you are not, and I am, I beg leave to say that I have no intention of letting Rodman leave our employ, now that he has got into it, and proved himself such a valuable railroad man. He sha'n't go, even if I have to make him 'master of something,' as you suggest, in order to retain his services. All that I want him to do is to visit Euston and become reconciled to his uncle. I am certain the dear old gentleman has forgotten by this time that he ever spoke an unkind word to his nephew, and is deeply grieved that he does not return to him. However, so long as Rodman's pride will not permit him to make the first advances towards a reconciliation, I will do my best to act as mediator between them. Then I shall expect our young fireman to appear in Euston as quickly as possible after receiving Major Appleby's invitation, even if he has to leave his beloved number 10 for a time to do so."

"All right, sir, I will," laughed Rod, "and I thank you ever so much for taking such an interest in me and my affairs."

"My dear boy," replied the President, earnestly, "you need never thank me for anything I may do for you. I shall not do more than you deserve; and no matter what I may do, it can never cancel the obligation under which you and Truman Stump placed me last night."

"It looks as though you and I were pretty solid on this road, doesn't it, Rod?" remarked the engineman, after the bridge had been repaired, and they were once more seated in the cab of locomotive number 10, which was again on its way toward the city.

"It does so," replied the young fireman.

CHAPTER XXXVIII.
A MORAL VICTORY.

The special was the first train to cross the Minkskill bridge after it was repaired and pronounced safe, and as it was followed by all the delayed passenger trains, the through freight did not pull out for more than an hour later. As the special moved at the rate of nearly three miles to the freight's one, and as it made but one stop, which was at Euston, where Eltje was left, President Vanderveer reached the terminus of the road in the evening; while Rod Blake did not get there until the following morning.

After devoting some time to the discussion of important business matters with Superintendent Hill, the President suddenly asked: "By the way, Hill, do you happen to have a personal acquaintance with a young fireman in our employ named Rodman Blake?"

"Yes, indeed I have," replied the Superintendent, and he related the incidents connected with the first meeting between himself and Rod. He also told of the imputation cast upon the lad's character by his private secretary. "In regard to this," he said, "I have been awaiting your return, before taking any action, because my secretary came to me with your recommendation. After Brown finished with the matter of the freight thieves, I sent him to Euston to make a thorough investigation of this charge against young Blake, and here is his report."

President Vanderveer read the report carefully, and without comment, to the end; but a pained expression gradually settled on his face. As he handed it back, he said, "So Brown thinks Appleby did it himself?"

"He has not a doubt of it," replied Mr. Hill.

"Well," said the President, "I am deeply grieved and disappointed; but justice is justice, and the innocent must not be allowed to suffer for the guilty, if it can be helped. I am going to Euston to-night, and I wish that, without mentioning this affair to him, you would send Appleby out there to see me in the morning."

"Very well, sir," replied the Superintendent, and then they talked of other matters.

In the meantime, during the long run in from the Minskill bridge, Rod had plenty of time to think over his recent interview with President Vanderveer. He recalled all the kindness shown him by his uncle, and realized now, what he had not allowed himself even to suspect before, that a selfish pride had been the motive of his whole course of action, ever since that unfortunate bicycle race. Pride had driven him from his uncle's house. Pride had restrained him from letting that uncle know where he was, or what he was doing. Even now, though he knew that his dear mother's only brother was willing and anxious to receive him again, pride forbade him to go to him. Should he continue to be the slave of pride, and submit to its dictates? or should he boldly throw off its yoke and declare himself free and independent? "Yes, I will," he said aloud; "I won't give in to it any longer."

"Will what, and won't what?" asked the engineman, whose curiosity was aroused by these words. Then Rod told him of the struggle that had been going on in his mind, and of the decision he had just reached. When he finished, the other exclaimed: "Right, you are, lad! and True Stump thinks more of you for expressing those sentiments than he did when he saw you board the special last night, and that is saying a good deal. To fight with one's own pride and whip it, is a blamed sight harder thing to do than anything else that I know of in this world."

They had already passed Euston, and Rod could not have left his post of duty then, even if they had not; but he determined to return on the very first train from the city, and seek a complete reconciliation with his uncle.

The day express had already left when the freight got in, and so he was obliged to wait for an excursion train that was to go out an hour later. It was made up of several coaches and a baggage car; but Rod did not care to ride in any of these. He already felt more at home on the locomotive than on any other part of the train, and so he swung himself into the cab, where he was cordially welcomed by the engineman and his assistant. They were glad of the chance to learn from him all the particulars of what had happened up the road during the great storm, and plied him with questions.

In spite of their friendliness, and of his recent resolution, Rod could not help feeling some uneasiness at the sight of Snyder Appleby sauntering down the platform and stepping aboard the train just as it started. He hoped his adopted cousin was not going to Euston. That is just where Snyder was going, though; and, having missed the express which he had been ordered to take, by his failure to be on time for it, he was obliged to proceed by the "excursion extra." He was feeling particularly self-important that morning, in consequence of having been sent for on business by the President, and he sauntered through the train with an offensive air of proprietorship and authority. Not choosing to remain in one of the ordinary coaches, with ordinary excursionists, he walked into the empty baggage car, and stood looking through the window in its forward door. The moment he spied Rod, comfortably seated in the cab of the locomotive, all his old feeling of jealousy was aroused. He had applied to the engineman for permission to ride there a few minutes before Rod appeared, and it had been refused. Now to see the person whom he had most deeply injured, and consequently most thoroughly disliked, riding where he could not, was particularly galling to his pride.

During the first stop made by the train, he walked to the locomotive, and, in a most disagreeable tone, asked Rod if he had a written order permitting him to ride there.

"I have not," answered the young fireman.

"Then I shall consider it my duty to report both you and the engineman, for a violation of rule 116, which provides that no person, except those employed upon it, shall be permitted to ride on a locomotive without a written order from the proper authority," said Snyder, as he turned away.

This unwarranted assumption of authority made Rod furious; and, as he looked back and saw Snyder regarding him from the baggage car, he longed for an opportunity of giving the young man a piece of his mind. His feelings were fully shared by the other occupants of the cab. While they were still discussing the incident, the train plunged into a tunnel, just east of the Euston grade. Here, before it quite reached the other end, it became involved in one of the most curious and startling accidents known in the history of railroads.

CHAPTER XXXIX.
SNYDER IS FORGIVEN.

As the locomotive was beginning to emerge from the blackness of the tunnel, and those in its cab were just able to distinguish one another's faces by the rapidly increasing light from the tunnel's mouth, there came an awful crash and a shock like that of an earthquake. A shower of loose rocks fell on, and into, the cab. The locomotive was jerked backward with a sickening violence, and for a moment its driving wheels spun furiously above the track. Then it broke loose from the train, and sprang forward. In another moment it emerged from the tunnel, and was brought to a standstill, like some panting, frightened animal, a few yards beyond its mouth.

The occupants of the cab, bruised and shaken, stared at each other with blanched, awe-stricken faces. They had seen the train behind them swallowed by a vast tumbling mass of rock, and believed themselves the only survivors of one of the most hideous of railroad disasters. Only Rod thought he had seen the end of the baggage car protruding from the crushing mass, just as the locomotive became released and sprang forward.

"The tunnel roof has caved in," said the engineman with a tone of horror; "and not a soul can have escaped beside ourselves. All those hundreds of people are lying in there, crushed beyond recognition. Oh, it is terrible! terrible!" and tears, expressive of the agony of his mind, coursed down the strong man's cheeks. Partially recovering himself in a moment, he said, "There is nothing left for us to do but go on to Euston, report what has happened, and stop all trains."

Rod Blake agreed that this was the engineman's first duty; but declared his intention of staying behind, and of going back into the tunnel, to see if there was not some one who might yet be saved. In vain they urged him not to, and pointed out the danger as well as the hopelessness of the attempt. He was certain that the end of the baggage car could be reached, and remembered the figure he had seen standing in it, as they entered the tunnel. He felt no trace of resentment against Snyder Appleby now; only a great overwhelming pity, coupled with the conviction that he was still within reach of help.

Finally they left him; and, armed with an axe from the tender, the young fireman again entered the dreadful darkness. Loose stones were still falling from the roof of the tunnel, and more than one of these struck and painfully bruised him. The air was stifling with clouds of dust and smoke. Only the lad's dauntless will and splendid courage enabled him to keep on. All at once the splintered end of a car assumed shape in the obscurity ahead of him. He heard a slow rending of wood, as one after another of its stout timbers gave way, and then, above all other sounds, came an agonized human cry.

How Rod cut his way into that car, how he found and dragged out Snyder Appleby's mangled form, or how he managed to bear its helpless weight to the open air and lay it on the ground beside the track, he never knew. He only knew, after it had been done, that he had accomplished all this somehow, and that he was weak and faint from his exertions. He also knew that he had barely escaped from the baggage car with his precious burden, when it was wholly crushed, and buried beneath the weight of rock from above.

Snyder had been conscious, and had spoken to him when he found him, pinned to the side of the car by its shattered timbers; but now he lay insensible, and apparently lifeless. Rod dashed water in his face, and in a few minutes had the satisfaction of seeing a faint color flush the pallid cheeks. Then the closed eyes opened once more, and gazed into the young fireman's face. The lips moved, and Rod bent his head to catch the faint sound.

"The cup is fairly yours, Rod; for I put the emery in my wheel myself. Can you forgive--" was what he heard.

Rodman's eyes were filled with tears as he answered, "Of course I forgive you, fully and freely, old man. But don't worry about that now. Keep quiet and don't try to talk. We'll soon have you at home, where you'll be all right, and get over this shake-up in no time."

A bright smile passed over Snyder's face, and glorified it. Then his eyes closed wearily, never again to be opened in this world. When help came, and the poor, torn body was tenderly lifted, its spirit had fled. His faults had found forgiveness, here, from the one whom he had most deeply injured. Is there any doubt but what he also found it in the home to which he had gone so peacefully, and with so happy a smile lighting his face?

Strange as it may seem, Snyder Appleby was the only victim of this curious accident; for the entire mass of falling material in the tunnel descended on the baggage car, of which he was the sole occupant. The hundreds of excursionists in the coaches were badly shaken up, and greatly frightened by the sudden stopping of the train; but not one was seriously injured.

President Vanderveer first heard of the accident at Major Appleby's house, where he was engaged in an earnest conversation with that gentleman, about his nephew and his adopted son. While they were still talking, a carriage drove to the door, bearing Rod Blake and the lifeless form of him whom the young fireman had risked his life to save.

After the Major had listened to the story of the lad who brought to him at the same time joy and grief, the tears streamed down his furrowed cheeks, and he exclaimed, "My boy! my dear boy! the pride and hope of my old age! Forgive me as you have forgiven him, and never leave me again."

"I never will, Uncle," was the answer.

At Snyder's funeral the most beautiful floral tribute was an exact copy of the Steel Wheel Club's railroad cup, in Parma violets, with the inscription, woven of white violets, "Forgive us our Trespasses." Directly behind the coffin, the members of the club marched in a body, headed by their captain, Rod Blake, whose resignation had never been accepted.

As for the young captain's future, the events on which this story is founded, are of too recent occurrence for it to be predicted just yet. That he will become a prominent railroad man, in some one of the many lines now opening before him, is almost certain. He finished his apprenticeship with Truman Stump, on locomotive number 10, and became so fully competent to act as engineman himself, that the master mechanic offered him the position. At the same time President Vanderveer invited him to become his private secretary, which place Rod accepted, as it seemed to him the best school in which to study the higher branches of railroad management. He is still one of the most popular fellows on the road, and his popularity extends to every branch of the company's service. Even Smiler, the railroad dog, will leave his beloved trains for days at a time, to sit in the President's office, and mount guard over the desk of the private secretary.

Not long ago, when the chief officer of the road was asked to explain the secret of Rod Blake's universal popularity, he replied: "I'm sure I don't know, unless it is that he never allows his pride to get the better of his judgment, and always performs his duties on time."

The Codes Of Hammurabi And Moses
W. W. Davies

QTY

The discovery of the Hammurabi Code is one of the greatest achievements of archaeology, and is of paramount interest, not only to the student of the Bible, but also to all those interested in ancient history...

Religion   **ISBN:** *1-59462-338-4*   **Pages:132**
MSRP $12.95

The Theory of Moral Sentiments
Adam Smith

QTY

This work from 1749. contains original theories of conscience amd moral judgment and it is the foundation for systemof morals.

Philosophy **ISBN:** *1-59462-777-0*   **Pages:536**
MSRP $19.95

Jessica's First Prayer
Hesba Stretton

QTY

In a screened and secluded corner of one of the many railway-bridges which span the streets of London there could be seen a few years ago, from five o'clock every morning until half past eight, a tidily set-out coffee-stall, consisting of a trestle and board, upon which stood two large tin cans, with a small fire of charcoal burning under each so as to keep the coffee boiling during the early hours of the morning when the work-people were thronging into the city on their way to their daily toil...

Pages:84

Childrens   **ISBN:** *1-59462-373-2*   *MSRP $9.95*

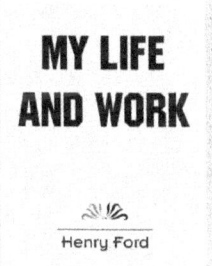

My Life and Work
Henry Ford

QTY

Henry Ford revolutionized the world with his implementation of mass production for the Model T automobile. Gain valuable business insight into his life and work with his own auto-biography... "We have only started on our development of our country we have not as yet, with all our talk of wonderful progress, done more than scratch the surface. The progress has been wonderful enough but..."

Pages:300

Biographies/   **ISBN:** *1-59462-198-5*   *MSRP $21.95*

The Art of Cross-Examination
Francis Wellman

QTY

I presume it is the experience of every author, after his first book is published upon an important subject, to be almost overwhelmed with a wealth of ideas and illustrations which could readily have been included in his book, and which to his own mind, at least, seem to make a second edition inevitable. Such certainly was the case with me; and when the first edition had reached its sixth impression in five months, I rejoiced to learn that it seemed to my publishers that the book had met with a sufficiently favorable reception to justify a second and considerably enlarged edition. ..

Pages:412

Reference   ISBN: *1-59462-647-2*   *MSRP $19.95*

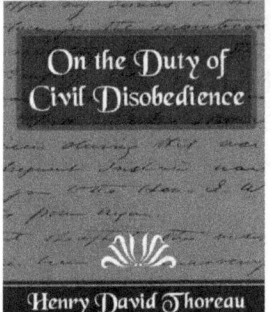

On the Duty of Civil Disobedience
Henry David Thoreau

QTY

Thoreau wrote his famous essay, On the Duty of Civil Disobedience, as a protest against an unjust but popular war and the immoral but popular institution of slave-owning. He did more than write—he declined to pay his taxes, and was hauled off to gaol in consequence. Who can say how much this refusal of his hastened the end of the war and of slavery ?

Law   ISBN: *1-59462-747-9*   **Pages:48**

MSRP $7.45

Dream Psychology Psychoanalysis for Beginners
Sigmund Freud

QTY

Sigmund Freud, born Sigismund Schlomo Freud (May 6, 1856 - September 23, 1939), was a Jewish-Austrian neurologist and psychiatrist who co-founded the psychoanalytic school of psychology. Freud is best known for his theories of the unconscious mind, especially involving the mechanism of repression; his redefinition of sexual desire as mobile and directed towards a wide variety of objects; and his therapeutic techniques, especially his understanding of transference in the therapeutic relationship and the presumed value of dreams as sources of insight into unconscious desires.

Pages:196

Psychology   ISBN: *1-59462-905-6*   *MSRP $15.45*

The Miracle of Right Thought
Orison Swett Marden

QTY

Believe with all of your heart that you will do what you were made to do. When the mind has once formed the habit of holding cheerful, happy, prosperous pictures, it will not be easy to form the opposite habit. It does not matter how improbable or how far away this realization may see, or how dark the prospects may be, if we visualize them as best we can, as vividly as possible, hold tenaciously to them and vigorously struggle to attain them, they will gradually become actualized, realized in the life. But a desire, a longing without endeavor, a yearning abandoned or held indifferently will vanish without realization.

Pages:360

Self Help   ISBN: *1-59462-644-8*   *MSRP $25.45*

www.bookjungle.com *email: sales@bookjungle.com fax: 630-214-0564 mail: Book Jungle PO Box 2226 Champaign, IL 61825*

QTY

The Rosicrucian Cosmo-Conception Mystic Christianity *by Max Heindel*   ISBN: *1-59462-188-8*   **$38.95**
The Rosicrucian Cosmo-conception is not dogmatic, neither does it appeal to any other authority than the reason of the student. It is: not controversial, but is: sent forth in the, hope that it may help to clear...
New Age/Religion Pages 646

Abandonment To Divine Providence *by Jean-Pierre de Caussade*   ISBN: *1-59462-228-0*   **$25.95**
"The Rev. Jean Pierre de Caussade was one of the most remarkable spiritual writers of the Society of Jesus in France in the 18th Century. His death took place at Toulouse in 1751. His works have gone through many editions and have been republished...
Inspirational/Religion Pages 400

Mental Chemistry *by Charles Haanel*   ISBN: *1-59462-192-6*   **$23.95**
Mental Chemistry allows the change of material conditions by combining and appropriately utilizing the power of the mind. Much like applied chemistry creates something new and unique out of careful combinations of chemicals the mastery of mental chemistry...
New Age Pages 354

The Letters of Robert Browning and Elizabeth Barret Barrett 1845-1846 vol II   ISBN: *1-59462-193-4*   **$35.95**
by Robert Browning and Elizabeth Barrett
Biographies Pages 596

Gleanings In Genesis (volume I) *by Arthur W. Pink*   ISBN: *1-59462-130-6*   **$27.45**
Appropriately has Genesis been termed "the seed plot of the Bible" for in it we have, in germ form, almost all of the great doctrines which are afterwards fully developed in the books of Scripture which follow...
Religion/Inspirational Pages 420

The Master Key *by L. W. de Laurence*   ISBN: *1-59462-001-6*   **$30.95**
In no branch of human knowledge has there been a more lively increase of the spirit of research during the past few years than in the study of Psychology, Concentration and Mental Discipline. The requests for authentic lessons in Thought Control, Mental Discipline and...   New Age/Business Pages 422

The Lesser Key Of Solomon Goetia *by L. W. de Laurence*   ISBN: *1-59462-092-X*   **$9.95**
This translation of the first book of the "Lernegton" which is now for the first time made accessible to students of Talismanic Magic was done, after careful collation and edition, from numerous Ancient Manuscripts in Hebrew, Latin, and French...
New Age/Occult Pages 92

Rubaiyat Of Omar Khayyam *by Edward Fitzgerald*   ISBN: *1-59462-332-5*   **$13.95**
Edward Fitzgerald, whom the world has already learned, in spite of his own efforts to remain within the shadow of anonymity, to look upon as one of the rarest poets of the century, was born at Bredfield, in Suffolk, on the 31st of March, 1809. He was the third son of John Purcell...   Music Pages 172

Ancient Law *by Henry Maine*   ISBN: *1-59462-128-4*   **$29.95**
The chief object of the following pages is to indicate some of the earliest ideas of mankind, as they are reflected in Ancient Law, and to point out the relation of those ideas to modern thought.
Religiom/History Pages 452

Far-Away Stories *by William J. Locke*   ISBN: *1-59462-129-2*   **$19.45**
"Good wine needs no bush, but a collection of mixed vintages does. And this book is just such a collection. Some of the stories I do not want to remain buried for ever in the museum files of dead magazine-numbers an author's not unpardonable vanity..."
Fiction Pages 272

Life of David Crockett *by David Crockett*   ISBN: *1-59462-250-7*   **$27.45**
"Colonel David Crockett was one of the most remarkable men of the times in which he lived. Born in humble life, but gifted with a strong will, an indomitable courage, and unremitting perseverance...
Biographies/New Age Pages 424

Lip-Reading *by Edward Nitchie*   ISBN: *1-59462-206-X*   **$25.95**
Edward B. Nitchie, founder of the New York School for the Hard of Hearing, now the Nitchie School of Lip-Reading, Inc, wrote "LIP-READING Principles and Practice". The development and perfecting of this meritorious work on lip-reading was an undertaking...   How-to Pages 400

A Handbook of Suggestive Therapeutics, Applied Hypnotism, Psychic Science   ISBN: *1-59462-214-0*   **$24.95**
by Henry Munro
Health/New Age/Health/Self-help Pages 376

A Doll's House: and Two Other Plays *by Henrik Ibsen*   ISBN: *1-59462-112-8*   **$19.95**
Henrik Ibsen created this classic when in revolutionary 1848 Rome. Introducing some striking concepts in playwriting for the realist genre, this play has been studied the world over.
Fiction/Classics/Plays 308

The Light of Asia *by sir Edwin Arnold*   ISBN: *1-59462-204-3*   **$13.95**
In this poetic masterpiece, Edwin Arnold describes the life and teachings of Buddha. The man who was to become known as Buddha to the world was born as Prince Gautama of India but he rejected the worldly riches and abandoned the reigns of power when... Religion/History/Biographies Pages 170

The Complete Works of Guy de Maupassant *by Guy de Maupassant*   ISBN: *1-59462-157-8*   **$16.95**
"For days and days, nights and nights, I had dreamed of that first kiss which was to consecrate our engagement, and I knew not on what spot I should put my lips..."
Fiction/Classics Pages 240

The Art of Cross-Examination *by Francis L. Wellman*   ISBN: *1-59462-309-0*   **$26.95**
Written by a renowned trial lawyer, Wellman imparts his experience and uses case studies to explain how to use psychology to extract desired information through questioning.
How-to/Science/Reference Pages 408

Answered or Unanswered? *by Louisa Vaughan*   ISBN: *1-59462-248-5*   **$10.95**
Miracles of Faith in China
Religion Pages 112

The Edinburgh Lectures on Mental Science (1909) *by Thomas*   ISBN: *1-59462-008-3*   **$11.95**
This book contains the substance of a course of lectures recently given by the writer in the Queen Street Hall, Edinburgh. Its purpose is to indicate the Natural Principles governing the relation between Mental Action and Material Conditions...   New Age/Psychology Pages 148

Ayesha *by H. Rider Haggard*   ISBN: *1-59462-301-5*   **$24.95**
Verily and indeed it is the unexpected that happens! Probably if there was one person upon the earth from whom the Editor of this, and of a certain previous history, did not expect to hear again...
Classics Pages 380

Ayala's Angel *by Anthony Trollope*   ISBN: *1-59462-352-X*   **$29.95**
The two girls were both pretty, but Lucy who was twenty-one who supposed to be simple and comparatively unattractive, whereas Ayala was credited, as her Bombwhat romantic name might show, with poetic charm and a taste for romance. Ayala when her father died was nineteen...   Fiction Pages 484

The American Commonwealth *by James Bryce*   ISBN: *1-59462-286-8*   **$34.45**
An interpretation of American democratic political theory. It examines political mechanics and society from the perspective of Scotsman James Bryce
Politics Pages 572

Stories of the Pilgrims *by Margaret P. Pumphrey*   ISBN: *1-59462-116-0*   **$17.95**
This book explores pilgrims religious oppression in England as well as their escape to Holland and eventual crossing to America on the Mayflower, and their early days in New England...
History Pages 268

www.bookjungle.com *email: sales@bookjungle.com fax: 630-214-0564 mail: Book Jungle PO Box 2226 Champaign, IL 61825*

QTY

The Fasting Cure by *Sinclair Upton* ISBN: *1-59462-222-1* **$13.95**
In the Cosmopolitan Magazine for May, 1910, and in the Contemporary Review (London) for April, 1910, I published an article dealing with my experiences in fasting. I have written a great many magazine articles, but never one which attracted so much attention... New Age/Self Help/Health Pages 164

Hebrew Astrology by *Sepharial* ISBN: *1-59462-308-2* **$13.45**
In these days of advanced thinking it is a matter of common observation that we have left many of the old landmarks behind and that we are now pressing forward to greater heights and to a wider horizon than that which represented the mind-content of our progenitors... Astrology Pages 144

Thought Vibration or The Law of Attraction in the Thought World ISBN: *1-59462-127-6* **$12.95**
by William Walker Atkinson Psychology/Religion Pages 144

Optimism by *Helen Keller* ISBN: *1-59462-108-X* **$15.95**
Helen Keller was blind, deaf, and mute since 19 months old, yet famously learned how to overcome these handicaps, communicate with the world, and spread her lectures promoting optimism. An inspiring read for everyone... Biographies/Inspirational Pages 84

Sara Crewe by *Frances Burnett* ISBN: *1-59462-360-0* **$9.45**
In the first place, Miss Minchin lived in London. Her home was a large, dull, tall one, in a large, dull square, where all the houses were alike, and all the sparrows were alike, and where all the door-knockers made the same heavy sound... Childrens/Classic Pages 88

The Autobiography of Benjamin Franklin by *Benjamin Franklin* ISBN: *1-59462-135-7* **$24.95**
The Autobiography of Benjamin Franklin has probably been more extensively read than any other American historical work, and no other book of its kind has had such ups and downs of fortune. Franklin lived for many years in England, where he was agent... Biographies/History Pages 332

Name	
Email	
Telephone	
Address	
City, State ZIP	

☐ **Credit Card**   ☐ **Check / Money Order**

Credit Card Number	
Expiration Date	
Signature	

Please Mail to: Book Jungle
PO Box 2226
Champaign, IL 61825
or Fax to: 630-214-0564

ORDERING INFORMATION

web: *www.bookjungle.com*
email: *sales@bookjungle.com*
fax: *630-214-0564*
mail: *Book Jungle PO Box 2226 Champaign, IL 61825*
or PayPal *to sales@bookjungle.com*

Please contact us for bulk discounts

DIRECT-ORDER TERMS

**20% Discount if You Order
Two or More Books**
Free Domestic Shipping!
Accepted: Master Card, Visa,
Discover, American Express

www.ingramcontent.com/pod-product-compliance
Lightning Source LLC
Chambersburg PA
CBHW08074725O626
47162CB00010B/3045